A Collectio
featuring the irrep … Fred Bunting

Fred!

Christine Bryant

Printed in the United Kingdom

ISBN: 9781916299948
First published in Great Britain in 2022

Right, said Fred

'Hello, Miss.'

Liz White looked down at the small boy balanced on the bicycle. Fred Bunting's face was shining with the cold, his tousled hair sticking out in all directions from beneath a woollen hat.

Liz had only lived in The Meadow a short time, but Fred and his mum had already popped by to introduce themselves. Now it seemed he was blessing her with a second visit.

'Hello again, Fred,' she said. 'How are you?'

'I'm okay, thank you.'

She smiled at him. 'You're a nice, polite boy.'

'Yup,' said Fred, modestly. 'It's just natural. You've been here two whole weeks now, haven't you?'

'Yes, I have. And it seems a really nice road to live in.'

Fred took a bite from an apple. 'That's what Mum says. She says it's a really nice road to live in. What you doing?'

'I'm pruning these roses.'

'Why?'

With a loud snip, Liz cut back a stem. 'If you prune them, you get lots of new shoots in the spring and hopefully, some nice flowers.'

'Oh.' Fred swallowed. 'Are you a teacher, Miss?'

Liz steeled herself. Being a teacher meant she was generally Teflon-coated when it came to children's questions, but according to the village, Fred's curiosity was off the scale.

'Yes, I am.'

'Mum said you was a teacher,' he said, casually. 'I said you wasn't a teacher, 'cause you don't look like a teacher, but she said you was.'

'And she was right.'

Fred turned the apple in his hand. 'We're doing about kings at school.'

She snipped another branch. 'Really, Fred? That's interesting. Which one?'

Taking another small bite, he said, 'Henry the Ninth.'

'I think you mean Henry the Eighth.'

'Ninth,' said Fred. He chewed carefully. 'He had loads of wives. Anne Bowling … Anna Clove …'

'Cleves. Anne of Cleves.'

Fred paused. 'They probably called it that in the olden days, but it's Anna Clove now.' He held out the apple. 'Want a bite?'

She shook her head. 'I'd better not, it'll spoil my dinner, but thank you.'

'We're having fish fingers today,' he said. 'And beans. I love beans.'

'Oh, so do I.'

He stopped mid-chew. 'I can save you some if you want.'

'No, thank you, Fred, that's very kind, but I have lots indoors. Perhaps you'd better run along now, eh?'

'HELLO, UNCLE PHIL!'

Fred's sudden ear-splitting cry jarred through Liz's head.

'Fred! Ssh!' Liz put a finger to her lips. 'You mustn't shout across the road like that.'

'I'M TALKING TO THE NEW LADY!'

Liz felt colour creep up her neck. *Really …*

'Fred!'

Oblivious to her protests, he cupped his hands and continued to yell. 'COME AND SAY HELLO TO THE NEW LADY!'

'Perhaps your Uncle's busy, Fred,' she hissed, watching in dismay as across the road a man stopped and turned around. 'You mustn't shout at people like that. It's very rude.'

As quickly as he'd begun, Fred stopped and turned to look at her. 'S'all right,' he said, simply. 'It's only my Uncle Phil. He's coming over.'

'Dear, oh dear…'

'Here he is,' said Fred. 'Hello, Uncle Phil.'

The man put out a hand and patted Fred's shoulder. 'Hello there, Fred.'

‘Hello, Uncle Phil. You haven’t been over to meet the new lady, have you?’ He looked up at Liz. ‘This is Miss White. She’s a teacher and she’s new. Miss, this is Uncle Phil. He’s not new, he’s old.’

Liz looked up into the face of her neighbour and gave an awkward smile. ‘Really, Fred. I’m so sorry, Mr … um … he shouldn’t have shouted out like that.’

Phil chuckled. ‘Don’t worry, honestly. And it’s Phil. Phil Williams. Nice to meet you.’

‘Nice to meet you, too,’ she said. ‘I’m Liz.’

‘Hello, Liz. Fred’s right anyway. I should’ve popped over before to introduce myself. How are you settling in?’

‘Very well, actually. I was just saying, it seems a lovely road to live in.’

‘Oh, it is,’ Phil said. ‘Nice and quiet -’

He glanced sideways at Fred. ‘Most of the time. And the neighbours are a great bunch, lovely and friendly. You’ll like it here … Fred, what *are* you looking at?’

‘Your watch. It says eleven o’clock.’

Phil’s grey eyes look puzzled. ‘And?’

‘And it’s eleven o’clock. You always have coffee at eleven o’clock, don’t you? That’s what you said. We had coffee the other day, Miss. Course, I don’t have coffee, ‘cause Mum says I can’t, ‘cause it’s got caffin in it and it’ll make me all hydro-active, so I have juice. And sometimes we have muffins. Uncle Phil likes chocolate chip muffins, don’t you, Uncle Phil?’

Phil gave an embarrassed smile. ‘Well …’

'And I like double choc chip,' Fred rambled on, 'but I'm not allowed them much 'cause Mum says they make me talk a lot, so I have strawberry. And lemon, sometimes, though I don't like them *so* much, 'cause they've got bits in them.'

He took a pause for breath.

'Thank you, Fred,' Liz said, quickly. 'I'll try and remember that.'

'That's all right, Miss,' he said. 'You can say which ones you like, 'cause I s'pect Uncle Phil's got some. He always has lots of muffins, don't you, Uncle Phil?'

Phil rubbed the back of his neck.

'Er … well … I do sometimes. Not lots, obviously, sounds like I'm eating them every five minutes.' He chuckled self-consciously. 'I do buy some. Now and again …'

'You buy *loads*,' said Fred. 'He's always got some in Miss, so I s'pect he'll have the ones you like, so we can all go and have coffee at your house, can't we, Uncle Phil?'

It was Liz's turn to feel embarrassed. 'It might not be convenient.'

'That's all right, Miss, Uncle Phil doesn't mind, do you, Uncle Phil?'

Phil gave an awkward smile. 'No … of course not. You're more than welcome, Liz. And you, Fred. If you want.'

Fred clambered off his bike. 'Yay!' he cried. 'I love having coffee at your house.'

‘Well, that’s very kind of you, Phil,’ Liz said. ‘But how about you both join me for coffee instead. If that’s okay with you, Fred?’

Fred looked thoughtful. ‘Got any muffins, Miss?’

‘Well, actually, I have,’ she said. ‘I bought some from the little bakers this morning. They looked so delicious I couldn’t resist them.’

Fred leaped up and down. ‘The ones from the bakers are *brilliant*! Aren’t they, Uncle Phil? We always have those. Last week, Uncle Phil ate two, all on his own!’

Phil swallowed. ‘Did I?’

‘Yup. You remember, you said it would be lonely in the packet all on its own, so you’d better eat it. That’s what you said.’

Phil coughed. ‘Did I say that?’

Fred nodded. ‘Thank you very much Miss, Uncle Phil and me would love to come into your house for coffee and a chat. We won’t chat much, ‘cause we do that a lot, but you and Uncle Phil can chat, ‘cause he’s separate, ‘n’ all. You told Mum you was separate, didn’t you?’

Liz felt a flush creep once more up her neck. She moved swiftly to open the gate.

‘Yes … yes, that’s right, but I’m sure we can find something more interesting to chat about. Let’s go in and I’ll put the kettle on.’

‘Cause if you two’s both separate,’ Fred went on, marching down the path, ‘you could get married, couldn’t you?’

‘Hope you like cinnamon and apple muffins, Phil,’ Liz said, desperately.

'Sounds good.'

'Miss …'

Liz took a very deep breath. '*Yes*, Fred.'

'If you do get married, my sister can be your bridesmaid and carry your bucket for you if you like. I can ask her.'

Liz decided it was time for a change of subject, and in her experience, the only way was to offer something more interesting.

Walking across to put the kettle on, she said, 'Actually, there was something I meant to ask you, Fred. Have you seen a little ginger cat about?'

Fred's eyebrows puckered. 'Is he little?'

'Yes.'

'And ginger?'

'Very. With white socks and ears.'

'Cats don't wear socks.'

'I mean he has white feet.'

'Oh. Can we please have the muffins now?'

'Of course.'

She set out the muffins and some plates. 'Help yourself, Phil.'

'Thank you, Liz. That little cat … it sounds as if it might be Napoleon. That's what I've called him. He's not mine exactly, I'm looking after him for a friend of mine. He's a sweet little thing.'

'We've got a picture at school, Miss.'

'A picture, Fred? Of Napoleon, you mean?'

Fred frowned. 'No. The Queen before. She was called Elizabeth, too.'

Liz smiled. 'My name's not Elizabeth, it's Eliza.'

Fred leaned across to whisper. 'It's Eliza, Uncle Phil.' Turning to Liz, he said, 'Uncle Phil asked me to find out your name, Miss.'

Phil gasped. 'Fred!'

'What? You did! He did, Miss.'

Flustered, Phil ran a hand through his curly hair. 'Fred, really … sorry, Liz, that's sounds awful. It's just that I run the neighbourhood watch scheme … if you're interested …'

'Oh yes,' she said. 'Yes, I'd be interested.'

Phil's eyes met hers. 'Wonderful. I'll drop over with a form, then, shall I?'

'Lovely … oh, look, there he is, the little cat.'

A small ginger cat perched on the windowsill, flicking its tail against the window.

Fred leaped to his feet. 'I'll get him!'

'Let him in, he can have some milk.'

Opening the window, Fred took the little cat in his arms and hugged him. 'It's him, all right, Uncle Phil. It's Napoleon, but he hasn't got his socks on.'

'He seems to like you, Fred,' Phil said, watching, 'maybe you could keep him. My friend can't have him back, because he's just moved into a flat and he's not allowed pets. Only if your Mum agrees, of course.'

Fred beamed.

'Mum'll let me have him, 'cause she said I could have another pet. And she said I couldn't have another dog, not yet, 'cause they keep chewing up the carpets, so she's got to get a new one, and she said I could have a cat if I want, so I was going to have one of Matthew's at school. His cat's had nine and he says I can have the one with the wonky ear if I'm allowed, but if I'm going to have Nappy, I won't need to, so I s'pect Michael will have him, 'cause he's allowed n'all, but I asked first. So I can take Nappy if you want. I'll look after him.'

Phil stared.

'Right. Well, that's fine then, Fred. I'm sure he'll love living with you. We all need someone to look after us, and it sounds like you're just the man for the job.'

Fred gave a sigh of pleasure. 'Well,' he said, airily, 'cats do like me. And dogs. It's just natural. I'll take him and I can bring him when I come down and see you. And you, Miss, though o'course, you won't need Nappy any more, 'cause you got Uncle Phil.'

Liz tried to say something, but nothing came out.

'I'll take him home now, 'cause he's tired,' Fred continued. 'I'd better take this last muffin with me to eat on the way and you and Uncle Phil can have a chat about getting married.'

Getting quickly to his feet, Phil slipped an arm around Fred's shoulder. 'I'm sure your lunch must be ready now, Fred, how about you nip along home. Here's a bit of pocket money for you, but ask Mum before you use it for sweets, okay?'

'Thanks, Uncle Phil.'

'Okay, Fred. Now you run along. I'll probably see you later.'

'Bye!'

The slamming of the door echoed around the house.

'Does he always slam doors like that?'

‘I’m afraid so. Sorry about that, Liz. My sister calls him the whirlwind, but he’s a good lad.’

‘Think I’m going to like living in this road,’ she said. ‘Sugar?’

‘Just milk, please. Yes, it’s a nice area. There’s some nice restaurants around here, too. Maybe we could try one … one evening, perhaps? If you’d like?’

Liz slowly lowered her cup. ‘I’d like that, Phil. Thank you.’

Outside by the front gate, Fred slipped Napoleon into his jacket. ‘It worked all right, Nappy, but we got out just in time, Uncle Phil’s eyes were going all funny. He’s probably going to ask her to marry him, so I’d better ask Lucy if she’ll be their bridesmaid. Come on, I’m starving.’

Fred and the Winter Ball

Fred stood at the window, nose tightly squashed against the glass. Beside him, his sister, Lucy, was doing the same. To anyone strolling idly past the Bunting household, the effect was a little startling.

'T'is,' said Fred, steaming up the window.

'T'isn't,' said Lucy. She tugged on Fred's arm. 'You promised.'

Fred folded his arms. Sometimes little sisters were hard work. 'I always keep my promises,' he said. 'Except when I don't. I said it was going to snow, and it is.'

Lucy returned to the window. 'Are the flakes very tiny?'

'Yup. You can't see the snowflakes yet, because they're so small. They've got to grow first. They're going to get bigger soon.'

'Can you see them?'

'Yup, but I'm older than you, so my eyes are bigger.'

Lucy suddenly leaped into the air. 'I see one! I see one!'

Fred, who up to that moment had seen no sign of snow whatsoever, put his hands on the window, and stared. To his delight, a damp, delicate snowflake fluttered down past the sill. 'Told you.'

Lucy continued to hop up and down. 'It's snowing! It's snowing!'

'Course,' said Fred. 'I promised, didn't I? It's like I said. I expect by tomorrow there'll be loads and we'll have to dig our way out. Course, if there's real loads, we might have to wait till they bring a big snowplough, and then they'll drive it in the gate and knock the front door down so we can be rescued, and there'll be snow everywhere and we'll have to move somewhere else.'

'There's another one!'

Fred nodded, sagely. 'That's two, then,' he said. 'It's definite.'

Lucy gave him a hug. 'Thank you, Freddie, for making it snow.'

'S'all right,' Fred said, airily. 'It's what brothers are for.'

Turning back to the window, he watched with satisfaction as two snowflakes became four, then eight, then a slow flurry.

'Looks like it's in for the dalmatian,' he said knowledgeably, as the flakes thickened. 'Better go and check on Nan and Grandad.'

In the cheery warmth of his garden workshop, Frank Bunting was blowing an imaginary clarinet. Eyes closed, his fingers caressed the keys, as Rhapsody in Blue filled his senses.

He was playing to the standard he was convinced he would have achieved had he not given up lessons as a child. His childhood neighbour, Montague Herbert, had been an accomplished amateur player, but for the young Frank Bunting, clarinet lessons could not compete with conkers and knock-down Ginger.

Lifting his make-believe clarinet into the air, Frank tootled a final flourish and waited patiently for the orchestra to join him.

'What you doing, Grandad?'

Fred was in the doorway, staring at him. Shaken into reality, Frank's imaginary clarinet dissolved and he pretended to flex his fingers.

'Just loosening up the old fingers, Fred,' he said, leaning across to switch off the radio.

'Is it your Arthur Rightus again, Grandad?'

'Fraid so, lad,' he said. 'This cold weather plays it up a bit. Now, how are you?'

'I'm ok. I've just come to check on you. I've checked Nan.'

'Have you? Why's that, then?'

Fred stared at him. 'Because of the snow, Grandad. It said on the telly you've got to check old people when it snows.'

Walking across, he peered at Frank, then grasped Frank's arm and wiggled it. 'Looks ok,' he murmured. He looked down at Frank's feet, then at his tummy, then leaned slightly outward to study his ears. 'D'you know you've got hair in your ears, Grandad?'

'I know,' said Frank. 'It keeps them warm in this weather.'

'That's brilliant.'

'Thank you, Fred,' said Frank, seriously. 'So, when exactly is this snow due, then?'

Fred giggled. 'It's here, Grandad. It started with two flakes and then it was four, and then it was eight, but now I've lost count.'

Frank turned to the window. Large fluffy flakes were pouring from the sky as though someone had unzipped the clouds.

'Well, I'm blowed,' he said. 'This is a turnup for the book.'

'Do books have turnups, Grandad?'

Still reeling from the ecstasy of Rhapsody in Blue, Frank had quite forgotten Fred's enquiring mind. On an average day, his grandson had enough curiosity for the entire feline population and enough questions to try the patience of a saint.

'Yes,' he said, quickly. 'Um … do you know, Fred, no two snowflakes are alike. That means every snowflake is different.'

'Wow! How d'you know?'

'Because scientists have studied them and they're all similar shapes, but very different patterns.'

'Why?'

Frank closed his eyes. He'd heard a snippet about snowflakes on the radio a few weeks back, but hadn't really been paying attention. Now he was wishing he'd listened to the rest of it. As a general rule, he believed in answering children's questions, but not when your grandson thought you were the person who compiled the questions for Mastermind.

He moved toward the window and cupped his hand to his ear. 'Was that your Nan I heard calling?'

'No.'

'Sure?' He gazed up the garden. The snow had already settled on the lawn like a white quilt. 'I say, look, there's enough snow to make a snowman already. Where's Lucy, in with your Nan? Go and fetch her and we'll build a snowman.'

'Ok, Grandad.' Fred opened the door. 'And then will you tell me about the snowflakes?'

'I certainly will,' he said.

Frank watched as Fred walked up the path and then he rushed to his phone, praying he would get a signal, and hopefully the answer to why snowflakes were different patterns.

It snowed all day and all night and by the next morning, the world looked a different place. Square things were round and round things were just little wavy lines.

In the Bunting household, Fred stood in the living room, staring out into the front garden through his new binoculars. He'd watched *The Snowman* three times now and if his own personal snowman even thought about moving, Fred was going to know about it.

He was keeping an especially careful eye on the frozen swede he and Lucy had used for teeth, when he heard a scraping noise, and trained his binoculars onto next door's front garden.

Mr Douglas was clearing his path.

'Hello, Mr Douglas!'

Gerald Douglas looked up with a smile. He felt full of the joys of spring, even though it was still February. It was a leftover from the previous evening when he'd reached across to draw the curtains and noted with delight that the snow was still falling. This is it, then, he told himself, it was in for the duration. Bit of a late start, but could it be another '63?

1963. The winter to end all winters. Of course, that had begun on Boxing Day, but one never knew.

'Well, hello there, Fred,' he said. 'Enjoying the snow?'

'It's brilliant!'

Gerald tried hard to disguise a sigh of pleasure. He shouldn't be this excited about snow at his age, he really shouldn't. 'D'you know what, Fred? It is brilliant!'

'D'you want that snow, Mr Douglas?'

Gerald glanced down at the snow piled high along the edge of his garden path. 'No, Fred, you take it, it's all yours. Make yourself a snowman.'

'Brilliant! Thanks, Mr Douglas. I'm making loads of snowmen, in case one of them flies off.'

Gerald looked at him, but knew better than to ask. In his experience, Fred's mind moved in mysterious ways, and he didn't want to be the person to tell him that snowmen didn't really come to life. 'Jolly good idea,' he said. 'Just a minute, I'll get my wheelbarrow.'

'Are you going to the Winter Ball?'

'The what?'

'The Winter Ball,' Fred said. 'It's this afternoon, at the Village Hall. Are you going? You can come with us if you like.'

Gerald opened his mouth to speak … and then stopped. Every time Fred 'invited' him somewhere, he would begin his polite refusal with, 'Well, that's very kind of you,' which Fred took as an immediate acceptance and rushed off to tell everyone Gerald was going.

Of course, he didn't want to appear bad-mannered, but the truth was, he didn't want to go to any Winter Ball and however well-meaning, Fred was not going to trick him into it, so rather than answer, he tipped the last of the snow into the wheelbarrow. 'There you go, Fred,' he said. 'You've got enough there for a cracking snowman.'

'Thanks, Mr Douglas. Me and Lucy need to practise because they're having a snow building competition outside the Village Hall first.'

'Sounds good.'

Fred leaned closer to whisper. 'I'm going to make a snowman,' he said. 'And I'm going to make something else, as well, but I don't know what yet.'

'Good idea!' said Gerald. 'Why don't you make a snow car? That's what we used to make. Or how about an igloo? They're good.'

'Wow! An igloo sounds brilliant! But I don't know how to make them.'

‘Oh, they’re easy enough, it’s just a question of getting the blocks right, I’ll show you …’

Too late, Gerald realised his mistake.

‘Thanks, Mr Douglas! I’ll ask Mum what time we’re going!’

Gerald closed his eyes. ‘Don’t mention it, Fred, that’s what friends are for.’

At eleven-thirty, Gerald Douglas left his home and began the short journey down to the Village Hall. He’d managed to politely excuse himself from walking down with the Bunting family *en masse*, but had promised Fred he would meet him there.

Tucked into his inside pocket were The Plans. It was a long time since Gerald had made an igloo and he couldn’t face the look of disappointment on Fred’s face if his creation collapsed into a heap of blocks.

He was stomping up the High Street, when he bumped into Colin and Margaret Meredith. Their twins, Molly and Ben, were rolling a very large snowball. Bob, their dog, was snuffling in the snow beside them.

‘Afternoon, Gerald!’

Gerald gave them a wave. ‘Hello there, Colin. Afternoon, Margaret.’

‘You off to the Winter Ball?’

Gerald nodded. ‘I am indeed. Promised young Fred I’d give him a hand with the snow building.’

‘Then we’ll see you there,’ said Colin. ‘We’re having a go at a snow dragon.’

Gerald nodded again, watching as they walked off toward the Village Hall. A snow dragon? Thank goodness he'd looked up how to build an igloo, the competition was going to be fierce. He glanced at his watch. Just time to nip in for a bar of chocolate.

He turned to go into the sweet shop and almost collided with Frank Bunting.

'Hello, Gerry, stocking up on some fuel?'

'Fuel for the inner man,' said Gerald, laughing. 'I've been requisitioned. Young Fred wants me to help him build an igloo.'

'Really? What's that little monkey up to? He's asked me to help him build an exact replica of *The Snowman*.'

'Oh?'

'Oh, indeed,' said Frank. 'You try finding a green hat and a check scarf at short notice.'

Gerald rubbed his hands. 'Guess that lets me off the igloo, then.'

Frank patted him on the shoulder. 'No, no, old chap. I wouldn't hear of it. I'll sit this one out.'

'Oh no, you don't,' Gerald said. 'He's a dear boy, but it's got to be my turn by now. I live next door.'

'What about me? I'm his grandad. I'm never off Wikipedia.'

Chuckling, they walked off together towards the Village Hall.

Inside the hall, it was warm and cosy. At the top, a large table had been spread with a wonderful buffet prepared by the ladies of the W.I, who had done the village proud, yet again.

As Gerald and Frank arrived at the hall, Fred rushed to the door to meet them.

'Grandad! Mr Douglas!' he gasped. 'I hope you don't mind, but Molly and Ben need me and Lucy to help them build their snow dragon. It was Mr Meredith's idea and it's going to be brilliant! Mr Meredith's even made some wings out of Tar Pauline!'

'No, of course we don't mind, do we, Gerry?'

'I should say not,' said Gerald, with relief. 'You go and have a good time, Fred.'

'Thanks, Mr Douglas! Coming, Ben!'

They watched Fred grab Lucy's hand and dash off into the snow to where Colin, Ben and Molly were hard at work on the dragon.

'Tarpaulin wings?' mused Frank Bunting, thoughtfully.

'Heavy stuff,' said Gerry, as he sipped his coffee. 'They'll need a wooden frame.'

Frank nodded. 'Certainly will. Colin's a superb teacher and I'd like to be half as clever as he is, but …'

'He's a thoroughly nice chap,' Gerald agreed. 'But even he'd admit, carpentry's not his strongest point, bless him.'

They shook their heads in unison. 'What d'you reckon, Gerry? Ten minutes?'

'Maybe,' Gerry said. 'If the wind doesn't get up.'

'Everyone outside! It's time for the judging!' Hilda Dunbar popped her head through the door. 'Better make it quick, it's getting warmer out here.'

'Oh dear,' said Frank. 'Not too warm, I hope. The youngsters will be disappointed.'

Outside on the small field, lots of wonderful snow creations had been built, and the builders stood proudly beside them, waiting for the judging.

It had been decided that Elias Woodward, successful entrepreneur and staunch supporter of village life should be asked to judge the competition, with assistance from Eugenia Barrow who had recently retired after thirty-five years with the Mobile Library.

They wandered slowly through the exhibits armed with clipboards and pockets full of rosettes, and mindful of the sun which had now peeped through the clouds and was starting to make its presence felt.

Faced with a long line of snowmen, the judges picked up the pace and ignored the sliding eyeballs and drooping noses. A snow plane was next and a helicopter, two versions of Spiderman and a Santa Claus, whose arm had melted clean off and was now laying in a small puddle by his sack.

Finally came the snow dragon, fiery and roaring in all its glory. Anchored around its body were Colin's home-made tarpaulin wings, and peeping from its mouth, several layers of coloured crepe paper in the shape of flames. Claws had been fashioned from brazil nuts and marshmallow bananas had been arranged in its mouth for teeth.

'Very scary,' Elias remarked, as they drew level with Fred, Lucy and the beaming Meredith family.

'And delicious,' said Eugenia.

As they watched, one of the dragon's eggshell eyes slipped slowly down the its nose and plopped to the ground. It rolled in the slight breeze and landed at

Eugenia's feet. Leaning down, she popped it back into place, and then the judges moved on.

Moments later, a puff of wind picked up the dragon's wings and lifted them slightly into the air.

'Oh Lord,' said Frank Bunting watching nearby, as the wings sank slowly down again. 'The wings are off. Hold onto your hats.'

Another gust sent the wings flying upright as if poised for take-off and as the judges turned, the crepe paper shivered like flames.

The judges nodded, and as Elias awarded everyone a runner-up prize, Eugenia walked across and placed the first prize rosette before the dragon.

Cheers and applause rang around the field. Standing behind the dragon for a photograph with the children, Colin was suddenly smothered by tarpaulin wings that blew him over and then disintegrated.

'Sorry, kids,' Colin said, as they helped him to his feet. 'Didn't last very long, I'm afraid.'

'It doesn't matter, Dad,' Ben cried, joyfully. 'They were brilliant!'

'You're the best dad in the whole wide world,' said Molly, hugging him.

Colin gasped with pleasure. Finally, he'd created something wonderful from his carpentry. 'That's what dads are for,' he croaked.

Later that afternoon, The Winter Ball was in full swing, and most of the younger villagers were on the dance floor twisting and turning in spooky movements to the sounds of 'The Monster Mash.'

'Come on, Grandad! Come on, Mr Douglas!' Fred dragged at their hands. 'Mum says you must know this one, it's from the olden days!'

Gerald and Frank looked with one accord at Grace Bunting, Fred's mum, who was giggling.

'If I'm not there in ten minutes, start without me,' Gerald said. 'I'm having another one of these scrumptious sausage rolls.'

'Oh, and me,' said Frank. 'And I must have another one of these scones. You carry on, Fred, there's a good lad.'

They watched with relief as he walked off.

Minutes later, he was back. 'We're here, Grandad.'

Frank turned to see Fred and Lucy, standing before him expectantly. Ben and Molly were with them, as were several of the other children.

'I told Ben and Molly about the snowflakes,' Fred went on. He turned to his friends. 'Snowflakes are all different, you know. There's no two the same. And my Grandad knows why and he's going to tell us all about it, because he knows everything.'

It was then Frank remembered. *Snowflakes*. He hadn't been able to get a signal, and he'd clean forgotten about checking on his laptop indoors. 'Well, I don't know everything.'

'You *do,*' said Fred. 'He does,' he added, nodding at his friends, who crowded around, eager to hear more. 'Is it all right if they listen, Grandad?'

The slice of cake in Frank's hand started to wilt. 'Um …'

'Fred?' Colin Meredith stepped to his side. 'Why don't we let Grandad finish his cake. I'll tell you.'

Fred gasped. 'D'you know as well, Mr Meredith?'

'Well, I didn't,' said Colin. 'But your Grandad told me this afternoon. I often ask him things. Now, this is why they're different patterns …'

He went on to tell the children all about changing temperatures through the atmosphere and different levels of moisture.

'Thanks for that, Colin,' Frank said, as the children rushed off.

'We were saying earlier what a clever chap you are,' said Gerry. 'I didn't have a clue.'

Still bursting with happiness after being called the best dad in the world, Colin beamed.

'Think nothing of it,' he said. 'It's what friends are for.'

Fred and The Maggie May

‘It’s going to be brilliant,’ Fred said. ‘What d’you think, Mr Douglas?’

Gerald Douglas peered over the fence at Fred’s sailboat made from a washing up liquid bottle. ‘I’m sure it’ll be absolutely splendid. Where are you going to put the sail?’

‘On the mast.’

‘And where are you going to put the mast?’

‘I’m going to make a hole in the bottom, and fix the mast with sticky tape.’

‘I see.’ Gerald scratched his chin. Fred Bunting was a good lad, cheerful, intelligent, and apt to ask rather a lot of questions. He had that look now and Gerald moved swiftly to stem the flow. ‘D’you know,’ he said, ‘it might be a better idea to put a large blob of sticky tack in the bottom and push the mast into that.’

Fred's eyes widened. 'Wow, that's a well cool idea.'

Gerald suddenly visualised Fred telling everyone why his boat had sunk. 'Though not too big a blob, of course,' he said, hastily, 'or it might sink.'

'Wow, Mr Douglas, you know loads,' said Fred. 'How big's a blob?'

'Well, you know, a blob. Like you squash between your fingers.'

'My fingers are smaller than yours. Shall I use two blobs?'

Gerald took a deep breath. And so it begins, he told himself. Quickly, he said, 'If you really want to enter the Summer Gala, Fred, I have a sailing boat you can borrow.'

'Wow, thanks, Mr Douglas, that'll be brilliant! We can sail it together!'

'Oh, I wasn't actually …'

'I'll tell Mum! She's making a picnic to take with us and we're having sausage rolls and pork pies and quiches and cakes and loads of other stuff and she'll have to make more now but she won't mind. Bye, Mr Douglas!'

Shell-shocked, Gerald hung onto the garden fence, debating the wisdom of allowing Fred to come within damaging distance of The Maggie May.

The Summer Gala. It was nothing too organised, nothing too fancy, and no kind of competition to The Henley Regatta, just an enjoyable gathering of the village in the park to sail boats on the lake. There would be refreshments on the green, a brass band in the pavilion and if everything went according to plan, a nice bit of sunshine.

In the kitchen of his home, Gerald finished a light clean of The Maggie May and put on the kettle. Pointless cleaning it really, he thought, if it was going on the lake, especially via Fred, but at least it would start out gleaming.

Gerald had loved boats for as long as he could remember. Unfortunately, the moment he had set foot on a real one, he was so horrendously seasick, even a local ferry trip was a nightmare. His dream of sailing the seven seas was relegated to the cupboard of unfulfilled wishes, where it sat with his ambitions to be a rock star, which had also come to nothing, despite a creditable singing voice and the right 'threads'.

It wasn't until his sixtieth birthday that his love of sailing was rekindled, when a chance visit to a charity shop brought The Maggie May into his life. She was a glamorous sailing boat in a sorry state, but the moment he saw her, Gerald was smitten. Here at last was the boat of his dreams and he would never be seasick again.

For weeks he worked to restore her to her former glory. Walking across, Gerald stared at her. She was beautiful. And he'd just told Fred he could sail her in the gala.

A sinking feeling washed over him, which for the owner of a sailing vessel was not ideal.

Everything will be fine, he told himself. You'll be there to supervise. Everything will be fine.

Iris Speed met Fred as she was walking down to the village on the morning of the gala. It was cloudy, with spits and spots of rain, but the sun was trying to break through and Iris was keeping her fingers crossed. Today she was sailing The Morning Glory.

'Hello, Mrs Speed,' Fred said, cheerfully. 'Are you going to the gala? Me and Mr Douglas are bringing The Maggie May.'

'The Maggie May? That sounds wonderful,' said Iris. 'Is Mr Douglas a Rod Stewart fan?'

'Who's Rod Stewart?'

Iris told him all about her teenage crush. 'He's a very famous rock star,' she said. 'I've got lots of his music. Anyway, I must be off. I've got to give The Morning Glory a check-over before this afternoon. I'll see you there. Bye, Fred.'

'Bye, Mrs Speed!'

Iris smiled as she watched Fred cycle off. He was a good boy, but she couldn't help feeling Gerald was being very brave letting him near The Maggie May.

The dog arrived shortly before the ducks, but somehow The Maggie May survived. Bursting through the undergrowth beside the boating lake as Fred proudly carried the glistening boat, the dog veered away from its owner and made a beeline straight for him.

It was a phenomenon known locally as 'the Fred effect' and came as no surprise to his family and most of the village looking on.

'Hello, Pickle!' Fred cried, as the enormous dog almost bowled him over. 'Hello, boy! This is Pickle,

Mr Douglas. He's called Pickle 'cause he's brown and splodgy.'

Suddenly realising The Maggie May could become equally brown and splodgy, Gerald bent to rescue it and lift it aloft.

'He's lovely,' he said. 'Let's get on and sail the boat, shall we?'

He passed the boat to Fred who, to his delight, cradled it as if it were a new born babe. Crouching down to the water's edge, he released her gently.

Almost at once, two ducks began to peck at it. 'Good heavens,' said Gerald. 'What's got into all the animals today?'

'It's probably because we didn't ask them, Mr Douglas.'

Gerald glanced at him. 'Ask them?'

'Yup. But don't worry. I'll do it.'

Walking across to the boating lake, he cupped his hands. 'Leave the boat alone ducks, it's Rod Stewart's. Course, Rod Stewart doesn't own it, Mr Douglas does, and we're going to sail it, so go over there in the reeds for a bit. Thank you.'

Gerald watched in stunned amazement as the ducks paddled furiously into the reeds.

'Rod Stewart, Fred?' he said. 'Where did he come from?'

'London.'

'Don't you mean Scotland?'

'No, he was born in London, Mrs Speed told me. He's a singer. She had a crush on him in the olden days and she said he sang about Maggie May, so that's probably how your boat got its name.'

‘Well, it wasn’t quite the olden days,’ said Gerry. ‘I remember Rod well as it happens. Used to be a bit of a singer myself …’

He could have bitten his tongue, but it was too late.

‘Wow, Mr Douglas, are you a singer?

Gerald gave a nervous laugh. ‘Everyone can sing, Fred. I was in a band, but lots of people were then. Let’s sail our boat, shall we?’

‘Ok.’

Gerald stared. Ok? Was that *all* Fred was going to say on the matter?

The next two hours passed very pleasurably, Gerald watching with pride as together with the other wonderful boats, the Maggie May glided through the water, turning gracefully in the light gusts of wind. It really was, he thought, a wonderful way to pass an afternoon.

‘I wish I knew how you do that, Fred,’ he said later, as they sat enjoying a delicious picnic.

‘Do what, Mr Douglas?’

‘You know, with the animals. It’s very clever. It’s almost as if they know what you’re saying.’

Fred fed the last of his quiche to one of the ducks. ‘They do, Mr Douglas. They’d say if they didn’t.’

Gerald opened his mouth to say something more, but thought better of it.

‘Hello, Gerry. Hello, Fred.’

They looked up to see Iris Speed smiling down at them.

‘I was just admiring The Maggie May,’ she said. ‘She’s a beauty.’

'Well thank you, Iris,' Gerald said. 'Picked her up in a charity shop and restored her.' He looked across at The Morning Glory. 'No surprise to see the Glory racing along. Have to be a pretty special boat to beat her.'

Iris nodded. 'My Geoff knew a thing or two about boats and ships.'

'We're doing about ships at school, Mrs Speed,' Fred said.

'Are you? That's splendid.'

'Yup. We're learning about how sailors used to live. They didn't eat quiche you know, they ate blue tack and stew.'

'I expect you mean hard tack. It's a sort of very hard biscuit. Horrible I should think. Not like this lovely picnic your mum's prepared.'

'Yup. These sausage rolls are smashing. Mum's made some for the dance in the Village Hall tonight. You coming Mrs Speed?'

'I should say I am,' she said. 'I wouldn't miss it.'

'Brilliant! Me and Mr Douglas are going, too.'

Gerald's tea went down in a lump. 'Oh, I won't be able to make it …'

'But you've got to! They're going to play it! Mums going to ask!'

'Play what?'

'Maggie May,' he said. 'Course, it'd be brilliant if Rod Stewart was singing it, but he's busy, so maybe you can sing it, Mr Douglas.'

'*Me*?'

'Mr Douglas used to be in a band, Mrs Speed and he knows Rod Stewart.'

‘I didn’t say I knew him, Fred, I said I knew *of* him. Most people do, he’s very famous.’

Iris put a hand on Fred’s shoulder. ‘I think Mr Douglas would prefer to leave it this time, Fred.’ She turned to Gerald. ‘Do come,’ she said. ‘I hear Percival’s got himself a Rod Stewart wig.’

‘Oh, bravo! Brilliant, Percy!’

Iris was up on her feet, clapping along with the others. Helped by a slightly hoarse throat, Percival Potter’s impersonation of Rod Stewart had been wonderful.

At their table, Gerald joined in with the applause. He was glad after all that he’d decided to come. Seated at a table with Iris and the Bunting family, he was having a very pleasant evening.

‘If you enjoy singing, you should pop along to our choir practice,’ Iris said.

Gerald shook his head. ‘Oh, I don’t know, it’s been years.’

‘We do all sorts. Lots of modern stuff.’ She leaned closer. ‘And we could do with a rock star.’

Gerald sighed. ‘Ah, those were the days. Or in my case, not.’

They shared a laugh, then looked up as Percy made an announcement. ‘That was a special request by the Bunting family in honour of The Maggie May, who nipped into first place in the last race of the day. Well done, Gerry and Fred!’

Fred beamed and held up a tiny cup. ‘It’s brilliant,’ he cried. ‘And I’m going to use it loads for my boiled egg!’

'Well done, Gerry,' Iris whispered.

'Thank you.' He raised an eyebrow. 'What a shame The Morning Glory developed a fault.'

She chuckled. 'It was worth it, just to see the look on Fred's face.'

Gerald glanced across at Fred, who was showing the trophy to his younger sister.

'You can look at it, Lu,' he was saying. 'But you can't touch, 'cause it's mine and Mr Douglas's and it's real gold and worth loads. Mr Douglas might use it sometimes for his egg, but he's letting me look after it, 'cause I know how to look after egg cups.'

'I can use it too!'

'No you can't!'

Percy slipped on his wig and took the stage once more and as the opening bars of 'Sailing' filled the air, Gerald got to his feet. 'I wonder if you'd care to dance, Iris,' he said, looking back at Fred and Lucy who were having a tug of war with the cup. 'Might be a little more … peaceful.'

'Thank you, Gerry,' she said. 'I'd be delighted.'

Fred's Easter

'Now there's a sight for sore eyes,' said Jacob Henry.

'Are your eyes sore, Mr Henry?'

Jacob looked at the small boy screeching to a halt on his bicycle. 'No, Fred,' he said. 'My eyes are fine. I count myself very lucky. I've got good eyesight for my age.'

'How old are you, Mr Henry?'

'I'm eighty-nine years young. Ninety on Saturday.'

'Wow! That's old,' said Fred.

'Certainly is. Seen a few things in my time.'

'What sort of things?'

Jacob knew Fred was one of those children who had an intellect way beyond their years, which was useful as they got older, but as his age, it could mean very long conversations.

'I've seen a great many things,' he said. 'Next time you're passing, we'll discuss one or two of them.'

'That would be brilliant,' said Fred, happily. 'I'm good at discussing. We're going to the Easter Fair on Saturday. Are you going?'

'I certainly am.' Jacob leaned down. 'Have you heard about the enormous Easter Egg that's going to be raffled? Mrs Buddle is donating it from her shop, she told me last week. It's huge, almost as big as you.'

Fred's face lit up. 'Wow!' he said. 'I'm going to ask Mum to buy some raffle tickets, so we can win. Bye, Mr Henry!'

Jacob laughed as he watched him pedal off. 'Bye-bye, Fred.'

Well, that was short and sweet, he thought. Usually, that young man had a multitude of questions. Just goes to show, chocolate was still top of the pops with kids.

He spent the next few minutes tending the raised troughs, where early bulbs were getting ready to flower.

Such a beautiful time of year, he thought. Springtime, new life, and lovely Easter traditions. He made a mental note to pop into the village bakery for some of their wonderful hot cross buns. And then of course, there was chocolate.

Perhaps Fred would win the giant egg. He had a sudden vision of him waddling down the road wearing the enormous Easter egg, arms poking out through holes in the sides. Where Fred was concerned, nothing surprised him. Chuckling, he slid the little fork and spade into his pocket, and started down the path.

'Mr Henry!'

Jacob glanced back, and for a second or two, he could scarcely believe his eyes. There *was* Fred, dressed as a chocolate egg, making his way toward him. Only a short while ago, he'd been talking about his amazing eyesight. Now he was beginning to wonder.

As Fred came closer, Jacob realised the obvious. Fred's suit was made of foam rubber.

'This is it, Mr Henry!' he said, as the suit wobbled and squelched from side to side. 'This is my costume for the parade! Mr Topping is going to be dressed as an egg as well, but he's a bigger egg. Miss Garfield is going as a chick, and Lucy is going as a chick as well, but she doesn't want to, she wants to go as an egg, same as me, so I said she can wear my costume if she wants, but Mum says her legs are not long enough and she might roll away.'

'I see,' said Jacob. 'Well, I think you look splendid. And I'm sure Lucy will, too.'

'We're all in the parade,' said Fred. 'Our teacher, Miss Flowers, says we'll look brilliant!'

'I can't wait to see it.'

'And,' said Fred, popping the tummy of his costume in and out, 'Chocolate is really really old, Grandad told me. It goes right back to the minions.'

'D'you mean Mayans, Fred?'

'Well, I expect they had it, too. And, in the olden days, they used to use it as money, and Stephen Fry made the first chocolate Easter egg ever.'

'I expect that was Joseph Fry, Fred.'

'Yup. *And*, there's going to be an egg hunt after the parade, and there's going to be baskets and everything, and it's going to be at Elias Woodward's house, and everyone's invited and there'll be a buffy 'n' that.'

'Really? How delightful. I bet you'll be really good at the egg hunt, Fred.'

'Well, I don't *know*,' said Fred, thoughtfully. 'Sometimes I can't find my socks, or my shoes, but I think I might be good at finding chocolate, because I always find where Mum hides our eggs.'

'A very useful skill,' Jacob said, nodding.

'Yup. I've got to go now, Mr Henry. See you later. Bye!'

Another smile creased Jacob's face as he watched Fred wobble up the street. He was quite looking forward to Saturday.

What a lovely birthday, Jacob thought, as he stood in the spacious grounds of Buckswood Castle on Saturday afternoon. He'd had an enjoyable morning opening birthday cards and gifts that had arrived from friends and neighbours, then he'd attended the Easter Fayre and watched the Parade. Now there were the festivities at Elias Woodward's house to look forward to.

Elias Woodward was a very successful businessman, who had moved with his wife, Shona, to Buckswood Castle, a large, quirky house that boasted a turret with castellations.

'Lovely day for it,' Jacob said, as Elias approached.

'Certainly is,' said Elias, shaking his hand. 'I understand it's your birthday today, Jacob, so many happy returns of the day.'

‘Thank you.’ Jacob waved a hand in the direction of the table, where the Easter Egg hunt was being organised. ‘This is a good idea, Elias. Keep the young ones busy for a bit.’

‘That’s the general idea. Our children are all settled down these days, so it’s kind of nice to have the laughter of kids about again. It’s an enormous garden, so there’s plenty of room for the kids to search. Shona’s thoroughly enjoyed herself organising it all.’

Jacob looked about him. The house and gardens had been beautifully decorated with bunting and streamers and a magnificent arch of silver and gold helium balloons.

‘The kids’ll love it,’ he said, smiling.

‘No use having a place this size if you don’t use it,’ Elias said. ‘Anyway, good to see you, Jacob, I’d better mingle.’ He grinned. ‘Tea tent’s over there.’

It’s true what they say about giving and receiving, Jacob thought to himself, as Sophie Pimm poured him a nice cup of tea. This whole day was giving Elias and his wife so much pleasure.

‘Hello, Mr Henry!’

Jacob looked round. Fred Bunting was standing beside him. Gone was the foam rubber egg costume he’d had proudly worn in the Easter Parade. In its place, he now sported a superhero jumper, jeans and trainers.

‘Hello, there, young Fred. Enjoying yourself?’

‘It’s brilliant! The egg-hunt starts in a minute and I’ve got some baskets for me and Lucy and we’ll probably get loads.’

‘Excellent!’

‘And when we’ve finished, we’re all going in the hall for the buffy.’

‘Well I’ll see you in there.’

‘And if Lucy finds more eggs than me, we’re going to share,’ Fred said.

‘And vice versa, of course,’ said Jacob.

‘What’s that mean?’

‘It’s a latin phrase, meaning ‘the other way round.’ It means if you find more eggs than Lucy, you’ll share with her as well.’

Fred looked. ‘Oh,’ he said. He was quiet for a moment. ‘We’ll probably find about the same anyway.’

He turned to go. ‘Course, I get first pick if I find them. Bye, Mr Henry!’

How reassuring, Jacob thought, with a chuckle. Big brothers never change. Or big sisters, for that matter. He took a moment to remember his own siblings. Never find first pick, he thought, it would’ve been every kid for themselves in our family.

In a comfortable armchair by the window, Jacob watched the youngsters rushing about the grounds, laughing and shouting, and screaming with delight as they found the eggs.

In and out the trees, under bushes, wedged into flowerpots, even pushed into crevices in the walls and fencing, there seemed to be an endless supply of eggs to be found, but it didn’t take very long for determined children from the village to exhaust the supply. Yelling happily, they arrived in the hall with their baskets for the eggs to be counted. The child with the most eggs would get first go in the lucky dip barrel.

'We've done it, Mr Henry!' said Fred, as he and Lucy showed him the eggs they'd collected.

Jacob looked down at the shimmering foiled eggs. 'So I see,' he said. 'Lucy's got lots of nice pink ones there.'

'Yup. I swapped her all the pink ones, 'cause she likes pink, and I don't mind having the blue and green ones. C'mon Lucy, let's get some food. Bye, Mr Henry!'

Jacob couldn't help grinning. Lucy obviously hadn't noticed the pink eggs were slightly smaller.

The buffet was delicious. Everyone in the village had brought something and soon, Jacob felt if he ate one more mouthful, he might burst.

At the far end of the enormous hall, the crew had finished setting up the largest inflatable toy he'd ever seen. It was like a long obstacle course. Children entered at one end, climbed over inflatable obstacles, through tunnels and up steps to an inflatable slide, shooting down onto a large, soft, bouncy square.

It was like bees to a honeypot. Children poured over it.

Jacob wandered over to watch.

'You coming on the slide, Mr Henry?' Fred asked, zooming in to land.

Jacob stared at the slide. It looked such fun. He couldn't remember the last time he'd been on a slide of any sort, but he'd never forgotten that wonderful feeling of flying through the air. The slide was soft. He couldn't come to any harm, could he?

'I'd love to have a go,' he whispered. 'Would you help me with the steps?'

'Course!' said Fred. 'I'll get my friend, Ben. We'll both help.'

He was as good as his word, and moments later, ably assisted by the boys, Jacob began the climb up the soft, squidgy steps.

'Jacob, are you sure this is a good idea?' John Bunting asked.

Jacob waved him away. 'I'll be fine, lad, don't you worry. The boys are doing a grand job.'

Slowly, he made his way up the steps and perched on the top. 'I feel like I'm on a mountain.'

'You ready, Mr Henry? We'll all go down together.'

Jacob roared with laughter. 'Righto, lads. Off we go!'

In a rush of sublime happiness, he let himself go and they slid to the bottom. All too soon, it was over.

For a moment Jacob sat at the bottom of the slide, eyes closed.

John rushed across. 'Are you all right, Jacob?'

'All right? I'm doing it again. Come on, boys. But this time I want to close my eyes on the way down.'

'Closing your eyes on the way down is brilliant, Mr Henry!'

Fifteen minutes and three more exhilarating slides later, Jacob sat back down in the armchair, feeling at peace with the world. What a wonderful feeling. He'd been a boy again, down on the seafront, laughing and yelling at the top of his voice.

'Thank you, boys,' he said. 'That was the best present ever. What a lovely birthday I've had.'

'And it's not over yet.'

Carmel Prentice and her sister, Rose were approaching, pushing a trolley covered with a cloth. Sitting in the centre, was a large cake glowing with candles.

'We thought we'd bring the cake to you,' Rose laughed. 'As you've been climbing Mount Everest.'

Amid a chorus of 'Happy Birthday', Jacob did his best to blow out the candles.

'I'll do the last ones for you, Mr Henry. You need a lot of puff for this job.'

Fred sucked in a long gasp of breath, then released it with some force, almost blowing the candles from the cake.

Jacob smiled. 'I appreciate that, Fred, thank you very much.'

'That's ok. I am good at blowing candles, it's just natural.'

'Come along, Fred,' said John, grinning at Jacob. 'They're about to draw the raffle.'

'Another lovely day,' Jacob said, as he lifted his cap to Florence Garvey, who was just coming out of the sweet shop.

'It's just beautiful,' said Florence. 'All these lovely bulbs coming up. Spring's in the air, you can feel it.'

'I'm surprised to see you in the sweet shop this morning. Fred tells me you were the lucky winner of the giant Easter egg.'

'I was. I got them to break it up and give it to the little ones.'

So like Florence, he thought. She adored children.

'Anyway,' she said, 'I'm not a lover of chocolate myself. Why would you eat chocolate when you can have a bag of these?'

She held up a bag of liquorice allsorts.

'Now you're talking. Your weekly allowance?'

'Not necessarily.' Florence grinned and offered the bag.

Jacob picked a pink coconut wheel. 'My favourite.'

Florence gave him a glance. 'Mine, too,' she said, tucking the bag into her pocket. 'I think I'll just take the rest home with me.'

He laughed. 'Probably as well. I could eat them by the handful when I was a kid.'

'Oh, and me. Bye, Jacob.'

For a moment after Florence had left, Jacob looked in the sweet shop window. Why not, he thought?

Fifteen minutes later, he left the sweet shop with a small carrier bag. Well, it wasn't his fault they had so many of his favourites, was it? Aniseed balls, mint imperials, Pontefract cakes, lemon sherbets, cough candy twists and pear drops, to name but a few. It had taken Jacob longer to make up his mind than some of the children standing at the counter.

As he turned the corner into his street, Jacob found he was looking forward to sampling a sweet or two when he got home. Those flying saucers, now, he'd not had one of those for years.

'Hello, Mr Henry!'

Fred was riding his bicycle up the road toward him.

'Hello, there, Fred. Out for a breath of fresh air?'

'Yup. Mum says I had too much chocolate yesterday, so I've got to drink lots of water and get lots of fresh air.'

'Probably a good idea.'

'Did you have lots of chocolate, Mr Henry?'

'Not really, Fred. I don't mind chocolate, but I prefer sweets.'

'I love sweets.'

Jacob gripped the carrier bag. 'Well, maybe in a few days …'

'I like flying saucers, but you have to be careful with them.'

'Do you? Why?'

'Cause they've got sherbet in them. And it goes all fizzy.'

'Yes, it is rather nice.'

'*And,*' Fred continued. 'It's got cedric acid in it, but it's all right, 'cause you can have a little bit, but if you have too much, you can get holsters. I had a holster once and Grandad gave me some jelly to put on it that tasted like pineapples.'

Jacob bit his lip, nodding slowly. 'I see,' he said. 'Sounds like you have to watch flying saucers.'

Fred's stared. 'Have you seen a flying saucer, Mr Henry? My Grandad's seen a yufo.'

'You mean a UFO, Fred. Well, as a matter of fact, I did see something many years ago, when I was a young man.'

'What was it?'

'I don't know. It was just something bright I saw in the sky, travelling very fast indeed. Sometimes, you see things that seem odd, but there's usually a reasonable explanation for them.'

'Wow!' said Fred. 'You've seen *loads*.'

'Well, I am ninety. You do see quite a bit in that time.'

'What sort of bits?'

Jacob could feel another long conversation coming on, which normally, he wouldn't have minded. But today, the prospect of trying one of the flying saucers, cedric acid or not, seemed a little more important, and he didn't want to undo Grace's good work by offering one to Fred.

'I'll tell you another time,' he said. 'I must go, Fred. Bye-bye.'

Fred turned and cycled off. 'Bye, Mr Henry!'

The flying saucer was every bit as good as Jacob remembered. The rice paper coating quickly dissolved, and as the sherbet fizzed and sizzled on his tongue, he gasped. Fred was right, it packed a punch. Hopefully, he wouldn't get a 'holster.'

He couldn't help laughing. Fred and his tales.

As Jacob sipped his tea, he decided he wouldn't elaborate on the UFO story any further if Fred asked. To this day, he didn't know what he'd seen in the sky that night, and he probably never would, but Fred had a fertile imagination and Jacob didn't want him having nightmares about flying saucers.

Rinsing his cup, he stood it on the draining board, picked up the key to his shed and set off down the garden. The spring sunshine felt wonderfully warm on his back. Halfway down the path, he stopped to pat the apple tree, feeling the joy of new life.

A sudden brightness caught Jacob's eye and he looked up. High above him, something was hovering, dazzling bright.

Hand cupped to his forehead, he squinted at it. What on earth?

He followed the blinding light as it rose higher in the sky, then abruptly vanished.

Opening a bag, Jacob stared down at a pink flying saucer, and smiled. It was probably just one of those silver balloons from the arch, reflecting in the sunshine until it had soared a little too high.

Or was it?

Fred at the Fair

'Mr Meredith!'

Colin glanced up. Racing toward him at an alarming speed down the path, was a small boy on a gleaming bicycle.

Fred Bunting.

Fred lived in the next road and was a frequent visitor to spend time with Colin's own children, Ben and Molly. He was a clever lad, blessed with the ability to see past the trees, straight to the wood, and so often, he was right. The simplest answers were the best.

Colin had tried to remember that this year, when his family had asked him to enter a competition in the Little Mopham Annual Show.

The show was a major date in the Little Mopham calendar. Originally agricultural and farming, it was now a Country Show and Fair and boasted all manner of attractions and exhibitions, displays of crafts and home produce.

But it was the competitions that brought in the crowds.

Last year had been a successful year for the Meredith family. Colin's wife, Margaret, had won two firsts in the jams and preserves and a second in the Victoria Sponge, and Ben and Molly had scooped first prize in the World About Us competition with their model of The Eiffel Tower in lolly sticks.

Competitions weren't really Colin's cup of tea, although he loved to cheer on the family and see them do well, but this year, he'd been persuaded that it would be a very nice thing for the family to do together.

Now, with the day of the Show finally here, Colin stood by the refreshment tent, his dog, Bob lying at his feet, waiting for Margaret and the children.

'Hello, Mr Meredith!'

'Well, hello there, young Fred,' said Colin, beaming. 'How lovely to see you again. You here with your Mum?'

'Yup, she's just coming. She's getting me and Lucy an ice cream.'

'Marvellous.'

'I'm getting banana and chocolate,' said Fred. 'Lucy's having lemon and sardine.'

Colin frowned. 'Lemon and sardine? Are you sure? I know Mr Whirl has added some new flavours, but …'

Fred nodded furiously, his hair flip-flopping about. 'I heard Mum say.'

Colin hoped he meant tangerine.

Propping his new bicycle carefully on its stand, Fred dismounted and bent down to stroke Bob, who at Fred's approach had stirred himself and trotted over.

Bob adored Fred. When it came to animals and small children, Fred Bunting had the gift. However grumpy and uncooperative the animal, however fretful the child, they were immediately soothed by his presence. It was a precious gift that other mere mortals like Colin could only admire.

That Spring, when Colin and the family had taken a two-week holiday in the Algarve, Bob had willingly stayed with the Bunting family.

'He always loves to see you, Fred,' Colin remarked, watching as Bob glued himself to Fred's leg, hanging on his every word.

'Cats and dogs do like me,' he said, 'it's just natural.'

'So, are you doing anything special at the Fair today, Fred?'

'Yup, I'm doing loads today. First, I'm helping Mum set up her pies for the show. She's trying some new ones this year.'

'I'm sure they'll do very well,' Colin said. 'I've tasted your mum's pies and they're pretty yummy. Mrs Meredith says they're yummy, too and she knows a lot about cooking.'

'*And*,' said Fred, 'I said I'd take Lucy on the Bumper Cars and the Coconut Shy and Dip the Duck and Ring the Hippo, and after that we're going to the sweet tasting.'

'Sweet tasting?'

'Yup. Mr Crabtree is running a stall this year and he's making his own sweets!'

'Good heavens,' said Colin. 'I wonder how he'll find the time. Isn't he doing Coco the Carnival Clown again this year?'

Coco the Carnival Clown was a regular feature at the specific request of Mrs Beatrice O'Grady, who loaned her fields for the Show and had rather a passion for clowns. She also had a passion for making costumes.

'No,' Fred said. 'Mr Crabtree can't do it this year, on account of his knee.'

'Oh, what's he done to his knee?'

'Don't know, but he's got a big bandage round it and he told Mrs O'Grady he couldn't do it this year.'

'Oh, I see.'

Colin suppressed a smile. He'd been persuaded to be the Clown once, but only once. For some reason, the jangling bells on the legs of the clown costume seemed to attract the teeth of every dog in the area and Colin never had a moment's peace. The only dog that had completely ignored the costume was his own dog, Bob.

'D'you know, Fred, it's lucky I've seen you,' he said. 'I was hoping you might find time to help me with an idea.'

'I'm brilliant at ideas!'

'I know you are. Now, the thing is …'

'I had a wicked idea only yesterday.'

'Did you? That's great. But the thing is …'

'I can tell you what it is if you like.'

Colin took a breath. 'I'd love to listen to your idea, Fred, but I was wondering if you could help me with my idea first.'

'What idea?'

'The idea I'm telling you about. It's something I've been working on, but I'm not quite sure about it. Have a look, see what you think.'

'I'm brilliant at being sure about things,' said Fred.

'I know you are. You see, the thing is-'

'And listening,' said Fred. 'I'm brilliant at listening, too.'

'You certainly are. Ok, here it is. Mrs M and the twins wanted me to have a go at a competition this year. You know, try and win something.'

For the first time since he'd arrived, Fred was silent. It was almost as if he couldn't quite believe what he was hearing. 'What are you going to do, Mr Meredith?'

'Well, therein lies my problem. I've tried my hand at making something for the New Inventions competition.'

The silence returned.

'You're the first person to see it,' Colin continued, enthusiastically. 'I haven't shown anyone else yet.'

'Oh.'

'You don't sound very excited.'

Fred stopped patting Bob on the head, and gazed at Colin. 'But, Mr Meredith,' he said. 'You can't make stuff.'

Colin felt affronted. 'What d'you mean?'

'It's all *right*,' said Fred, reaching into his pocket for an apple and taking a large bite. 'Grandad said some people are good at making things and some people are good at thinking things. Course, Grandad can do both -'

'What d'you mean, I'm no good at making stuff, er … things?'

'Well.' Fred leaned in to whisper. 'Everyone knows about your garden shed.'

'That,' said Colin, peevishly, 'was a design fault.'

'Oh.'

'And it was very windy that day. That could have happened to anyone.'

'Oh,' said Fred, again. He took another bite of his apple. At his feet, Bob gazed up adoringly.

'Anything else?'

'No,' said Fred. 'But don't worry Mr Meredith, 'cause you being a maths teacher, you're really, really clever and you know loads, and all that stuff about numbers 'n' that. Course, Grandad's good at numbers, too.'

'Of course.'

'He's not as good as you, though,' Fred continued. 'And he can't make rolling shelves, either.'

'Rolling shelves?'

'Yup. You remember, those rolling shelves you made for Ben and Molly. Ben says they're great. Whatever you put on them rolls straight off.'

'Oh.'

Taking a last bite of his apple, Fred put the core neatly into his pocket. 'So, what is it?'

'What's what?'

'That thing what you made. Can I see it?'

Colin looked down at his canvas bag on the ground and thought about the self-twirling spaghetti fork lying courageously inside.

With a sigh, he said, 'I'll let you see it, if you promise to give me your honest opinion on it without telling anyone else.'

'I promise.'

'Truly? It won't get about like my garden shed?'

'But your garden shed did get about, Mr Meredith. It got about all over Mrs Pope's prize dahlias and Mr Bernard's marrows, that's why everyone knows.'

Colin shrugged. 'Fair point,' he said. 'Ok then, I'll show you. Let me know what you think.'

Carefully, he unzipped the bag and produced the fork, wrapped in tissue paper.

'Wow!' said Fred. 'It's a spaghetti fork. A twirling one like Mum's got. But hers is not all shiny like this one.'

Colin's dreams crumbled to dust. 'Your Mum has a self-twirling spaghetti fork?'

Fred nodded. 'It's broken now, though, 'cause Dad used it for mixing paint, so I bet Mum'll buy this one!'

'Oh, well. I suppose that'd be something. Look, this is how it works.' Colin pressed the base. Nothing happened.

'Probably a loose battery,' he said. He moved the batteries about. Still nothing.

'Oh,' said Fred, watching, 'it's broken. Want me to take it to Grandad? Bet he can fix it. He can fix anything.'

Colin tucked the fork swiftly into his pocket. 'No thanks, Fred. I think I'll just forget about it for the time being. Only trouble is, I promised the family I'd have a go at winning something. Still, can't be helped. Off you go, Fred and enjoy the fair. Thanks for listening.'

'Bye, Mr Meredith!'

'Goodbye, Fred.'

'Mr Meredith!'

Colin looked up from his consolation cup of tea and Eccles cake.

Fred was riding towards him, waving wildly.

'Mr Meredith! I've got it! I've thought of a way you can win a prize!'

Colin shook his head. 'That's good of you, Fred, but I don't think…'

'But you've got to! It'll be easy, come on!'

With a deep sigh, Colin pushed himself to his feet and followed Bob, who suddenly seemed to have a new lease of life and was now trotting along beside Fred's bike.

'Ok, Fred,' said Colin, wearily, as they approached an open field. 'What are we doing here?'

'We're going to be a team,' he said and with that, he walked into the tent. Colin followed.

'Bob can be in the dog competition,' said Fred.

Colin looked down at the mongrel sitting between them. Bob was a dear dog and they all loved him very much, but he was never going to grace the pages of Doggy World. His coat was a mish-mash of colours and blotches, straight in some parts and curly in others and one of his ears crooked slightly to the left, though that, at least, was balanced by the bump on his nose. His eyes were slightly different colours, but were warm, gentle and loving.

'Bob? In a competition? What sort?'

'Most Talented Dog,' said Fred. 'It's new this year.'

'Look, I know you mean well, Fred,' said Colin, visions of yet another embarrassing spectacle looming, 'but Bob's not what you might call talented. I can't get him to sit half the time. Especially today, he's in one of his moods today. All he's done is snuffle, sniff and pull on his lead.'

'He is talented. Mr Meredith with Bob,' he said, to the lady behind the table.

'Class?' she asked.

'None, I'm afraid,' said Colin. 'But we'd like to try Most Talented Dog, please.'

The lady glanced over the table at Bob and then sympathetically back at Colin. 'Of course,' she said, and passed them a number.

Together they walked through the tent and out into the open field to join the others.

'Are you sure about this, Fred?' Colin asked, watching from the corner of his eye as a new Coco the Carnival Clown made its way slowly through the crowd, vainly trying to loosen two terriers from the trouser legs.

'Ladies and Gentlemen -'

Mr Jewel's voice over the loudspeaker system announced the Dog Show would begin in five minutes.

‘It’s ok,’ said Fred. ‘I’ve been telling Bob what he’s got to do. He knows.’

Colin closed his eyes. Another fiasco coming up. Fred was amazing with animals, but miracles?

One by one, the various dogs were put through their paces by their proud owners. With the exception of one, all could sit, lay down, roll over and hold out a paw, and much to Colin’s delight and disbelief, Bob played along very nicely. A select few did other tricks; a dalmatian balanced an egg on its nose for a full minute before eating it, a toy poodle did the cutest balancing act on its hind legs and with the aid of a bowler hat and a cardboard cigar, a bulldog did a passing impression of Winston Churchill.

Now, it was Bob’s turn. Grandly, Fred led him out to the front.

‘Flip, Bob,’ he said. Bob flipped over in a smooth roll, landing back on his feet.

‘March, Bob.’ Bob lifted one paw, then the other and marched forward.

‘Good grief,’ said Colin, watching in amazement, as applause rang through the crowd.

‘For his final trick,’ Fred announced, ‘Bob will…’

At that moment, before Colin, Fred or anyone else could react, Bob took off and charged across the field.

And so it begins, thought Colin.

Fred burst after him, yelling, ‘He’s after something, Mr Meredith! He’s a brilliant tracker!’

‘Since when?’

Followed by Fred, Colin and several by-standers, Bob ran straight for Coco the Carnival Clown, who had been standing in the crowd, watching.

Oh no, Colin thought, it's the bells on that silly costume!

Ignoring everyone and everything, Bob took one enormous bound, flew through the air and sent Coco the Carnival Clown tumbling to the grass.

Fred and Colin reached the poor beleaguered clown, just as Sergeant Rose jogged up to the scene.

'Right,' said Sergeant Rose. 'What's going on?'

'This brute attacked me!' The clown struggled to his feet. 'I was standing here, just watching, when for absolutely no reason, this -'

Going in for a final lunge, Bob had torn apart Coco's costume. Out from the voluminous trouser legs tumbled a variety of purses, wallets and other personal items.

'My purse!' cried Mrs Norman.

Harold Meakins crouched down to pick up a wallet. 'And that looks very much like … it is!'

'My necklace!'

Sergeant Rose turned his very serious attention to Coco the Carnival Clown.

'I can't understand it,' Colin said, as he polished the small trophies and stood them back on the shelf. 'I mean I'm not complaining …'

'Oh no, dear,' said his wife, passing him a cup of tea. 'Our Bob's a hero, tackling a criminal like that.'

'But that's what I mean,' said Colin. 'I mean, it's amazing that he did it, of course and like you say, he's a hero …'

'And he won two cups!' cried Ben. 'One for being Most Talented Dog and one for being so brave!'

'Well, of course,' said Colin, 'and he deserved them, but I mean, why? Why did he do it? He's not usually that energetic.'

'Because he's the best dog in all the world!' yelled Molly, flinging her arms about Bob's neck.

Yes, he is, thought Colin later, as he dug over his front garden. Yes, Bob is the best dog in the world, but …

'Hallo, Mr Meredith!'

Rocket Fred was approaching.

'Hello, again, Fred. Come to see Ben and Molly?'

Fred nodded. 'I want to show them my new model kit.'

'Excellent. They're in the kitchen. Go on in.' On a sudden whim, he added, 'Fred, have you any idea what got into Bob the other day?'

'Bob's a hero!'

'Absolutely,' said Colin. 'But I can't help wondering why he did it. I thought at first it was the bells on the costume, but he never reacted like that when I wore it. Other dogs did, but he didn't.'

'It wasn't the bells, Mr Meredith, it was the pie.'

'Pie? What pie?'

'Didn't you see it, on the clown's pocket? That big stain? That was one of Mum's steak and kidney. Bob loves Mum's steak and kidney pies.'

'When has he had one of those, then?'

'When you were on holiday in the All-grave and he was staying with us and I was training him,' said Fred, casually. 'Mum was trying out a new recipe and we had pies ever such a lot, so I saved Bob some, and I gave him a piece when he got things right.'

Stunned by the sheer simplicity of the answer, Colin watched Fred saunter into the kitchen, to be greeted enthusiastically by Bob.

So that's why Bob kept sniffing and snuffling, Colin thought, he could smell Grace Bunting's pie stall.

Lifting his garden fork, Colin plunged it into the earth.

The simplest answers were so often the best.

Fred and The Wishing Well

'Dad says our rose is going to have a load of bloomers this year,' Fred said.

Zinnia Pickles looked up. 'Who?'

'Our rose. Going to be covered in bloomers, Dad said. They're showing already.'

'Oh, you mean blooms, Fred,' she said, with a smile. 'Yes, well, that's quite likely. My roses are showing promise, too.'

Fred picked up his small fork and plunged it into the soil. 'It's really kind of you to help me with my school project. It's a shame Lucy couldn't come, 'cause she loves gardening, same as me.' He gave a sigh. 'But she's going to a party with her friend today.'

'Well, that's very nice,' said Zinnia. 'I'm sure she'll have a lovely time.'

'I love digging,' he said, as he plunged his fork once more into the soil. 'Here's one!'

'Well done.' She took the worm carefully from Fred's hands and put it into the bucket of soil.

'Napoleon likes digging, too,' he said.

'Napoleon's your little cat, isn't he?'

Fred nodded. 'Yup. He likes digging 'n' all, especially in Mr Douglas' garden next door, but Mr Douglas doesn't like him doing it 'cause he poos.'

'I see,' said Zinnia. Swiftly changing the subject, she said, 'Gardens are magical places, Fred. Where wonderful things happen.'

'What sort of things?'

She was prepared for this to be the first of a great many questions that afternoon. Fred's curiosity rivalled that of any cat she'd ever met, but he was a well-mannered boy, always willing to help, even if sometimes, it was more of a hindrance.

'Oh, lots of things,' she said. 'You can put the tiniest little seed -'

She ripped the top off a packet and tipped several minute seeds into her hand. 'Like these, into the soil, give it a drop of water and from that, a tiny seed will grow into a flower, and if that's not magic, I don't know what is.'

Fred nodded, solemnly. 'What other magic is there, though? Are there magic places where fairies live? Course, I don't believe in fairies,' he said, airily. 'But Lucy does and I bet she wants me to ask.'

'I'm sure she will,' said a voice.

Zinnia turned to see her mum, Marigold, walking towards them across the lawn. Pushing her fork back into the soil, she walked over to help her. 'Cup of tea, Mum?'

'Lovely, dear,' she said. 'Fred and I will have a little sit down on the swing. Come on, Fred. Now,'

Zinnia heard her say as she walked away. 'It's interesting you should ask about fairies, Fred …'

Zinnia smiled to herself as she looked out of the kitchen window, to see her mum and Fred in earnest conversation. He'll probably hear the old story about the woodnymphs one day, she thought to herself. She'd heard the story often enough over the years and she knew it by heart.

Mum had lived in this house and garden as a girl and she loved every inch of it. It was a pretty garden, unusual really, full of twists and turns and hidden places. At the very end, was a beautiful copse of trees, and if such a place existed, then, yes, Zinnia could believe Bluebell Copse was magical.

Filling the kettle, she popped it on to boil, set out two mugs, and poured Fred a glass of orange juice.

Bluebell Copse, she thought, as she waited for the kettle. She'd been a teenager when Mum had shown her the photograph her great-grandad had taken all those years ago.

Two little girls sitting happily on a large stone pot, swinging their legs in the sunshine. The little girls were beautiful and yes, their faces had an almost ethereal look, but somehow, Zinnia could never bring herself to believe they were woodnymphs.

'So, you see, Fred,' Marigold Pickles continued, 'there are lots of different types of life in a garden. In a moment, we'll pop down to Bluebell Copse and I'll show you the fairy ring.'

'Are there real fairies there?'

'Well, you never know,' said Marigold. 'There are lots of different things in life, but a fairy ring is where toadstools grow in a circle. Years ago, people used to believe that they were little seats for the fairies.'

'Of course, what they really are,' Zinnia said, as she arrived with the tea, 'are places where toadstool and mushroom seeds land in a spot they like and they send out very fine threads underground and more grow. It's all very clever, Fred. We'd be in a right old state without fungi.'

'We're doing about fungi at school,' he said. 'Toadstools 'n' that. And Miss said you must never ever pick them, 'cause some are poisonous and they have spots. My dad's got a spot on his chin, and he caught it when he was shaving, but it's all right.'

'Of course,' said Marigold. 'Now, let's go and look at this fairy ring.'

'Course, I won't catch any spots when I'm shaving,' he said, as they walked down to the copse. 'And I expect I'll have to shave quite a bit.'

'Here's the fairy ring, Fred,' Marigold said, smiling to herself. 'You see how they all grow in a little circle?'

Fred bent over to take a closer look. 'Five … six … seven,' he counted. 'That's enough for seven fairies. Or, if they're very small fairies, they could get two on each, so that's fourteen. I'll tell Lucy.'

He looked about him. 'I like Bluebell Copse.'

Marigold gave him a glance. 'So do I.'

'What's that?'

Zinnia walked across to a small stone wishing well. 'This is our wishing well,' she said. 'Of course, it's not a real well, it's only a stone ornament, but it does have a little dish at the top here, look, that fills up with water when it rains, so all the birds can have a nice drink. It's very important to give the birds a drink, even in the winter. They like a nice bath, too.'

'I like a nice bath,' said Fred, seriously.

Marigold slipped an arm about his shoulders and squeezed. 'Oh, Fred, you are funny.'

'My Nan says I'm funny,' said Fred, walking across to the wishing well. 'And I am very funny sometimes, it's just natural, 'specially when I tell jokes 'n' that.'

'Are you very good at jokes, then, Fred?'

'Yup.' He drew in a long breath. 'Why did the turkey cross the road?'

Zinnia and her mum pretended to look puzzled. 'No, we give up.'

'Because it was the chicken's day off.'

They all shared a laugh.

'Can you make a wish in this well?' Fred asked, peering into the tray. 'You know, throw coins in 'n' that?'

'Well, I suppose you could if you wanted to,' said Zinnia. 'But I don't know if it would come true.'

'I think it probably would,' said Fred, 'cause this garden must have a lot of magic in it with the fairy ring and everything.'

He reached into his pocket. 'I've got this button off my jumper. D'you think it would work if I threw that in?'

Marigold put a hand on his shoulder. 'I think it's quite possible,' she said, making a mental note to fish it out later and return it to his mum. 'And I'm sure the fairies would be glad of a button. It might be very useful.'

'Brilliant!' said Fred, and tossed the bright blue button into the dish.

'I made a wish the other day,' Fred said, as he peered over the fence.

Behind his newspaper in the garden next door, Gerald Douglas closed his eyes. So much for his quiet sit with the crossword. 'Jolly good,' he murmured.

'Don't you want to know what I wished for?'

'You mustn't tell people that or it won't come true,' Gerald said monotonously, trying desperately to concentrate on three down. The last clue. Why, he thought? Why is there always one clue I can't get?

'But how you will you know if it's come true, if I don't tell you what it is?'

Gerald lowered his paper. '*You* will know, Fred,' he said. 'That's the whole point.'

'Oh.'

He lifted his paper again and glared at three down. You do know it, he told himself, you know you do. You know that bit of information, but where have you put it? He rapped his forehead with his knuckles.

'Have you got a headache, Mr Douglas?'

Yes, thought Gerald, and thy name is Fred. 'No,' he said. 'But thank you for asking, Fred. I'm just trying to remember something, that's all.'

'What are you trying to remember?'

'If I knew that, Fred, I wouldn't be trying to remember it.'

Fred giggled. 'That's funny, Mr Douglas,' he said. 'You're funny, same as me. Miss Pickles and her mum said I was very funny, 'cause I told them the joke about the turkey. Do you want to hear the joke about the turkey?'

'If I must.'

'Why did the turkey cross the road?'

Gerald took a deep breath. It was evidently going to be a long afternoon. 'No, I give up.'

'Because it was the chicken's day off.'

Sitting in his kitchen later that day, Gerald struggled to understand why Fred's dreadful joke had so tickled his funny bone and turned him into a giggling fool. He could only assume the hours of frustration caused by three down had finally found an outlet.

He stared again at the crossword. One clue!

Gerald glanced at his laptop sitting innocently on the sideboard. How easy it would be to look it up on the internet. No, he told himself, you've *got* to remember it.

'Hello, Miss Pickles.'

Zinnia stopped halfway down the High Street and turned around. 'Well, hello again, Fred,' she said. 'How are you? And how's Lucy? Did she have a nice time at her friends?'

'Yes, thank you,' he said. 'My teacher says the worms you helped me collect for our wormery are brilliant, and she said thank you very much.'

'It was my pleasure,' said Zinnia. 'You can have a lot of fun in a garden.'

'I wish I had a magic garden like yours,' said Fred, wistfully.

'All gardens are magic, Fred.'

'But not like yours.' He gave a little sigh. 'I've looked everywhere, but we still haven't got a fairy ring. And I told Lucy about the fairies.'

Zinnia reached into her bag and pulled out a bag of toffees. Fairies? Had mum told him the story about the woodnymphs, then? Somehow, she didn't think it likely. 'Would you like a toffee, Fred? They're liquorice.'

'I love lickerish,' he said. 'Thank you very much.'

'Did you say you told Lucy about the fairies?'

'Yush,' Fred slurped. He moved the toffee to one side. 'I told her the story Mrs Pickles told me.'

Zinnia frowned. 'Which story was that, again?'

Fred moved the toffee back. 'The one about the two little girlsh.'

'Which two?'

'The ones who lived in Cotton Lee.'

'Oh, you mean the Cottingley Fairies!' Zinnia cried. 'Well, of course, you know they're weren't real, don't you?'

Fred chewed quickly and swallowed. 'Yup,' he said. 'Mrs Pickles told me. But Lucy said can we grow a fairy ring and we might get some real fairies.'

'Oh, I see.' Zinnia looked down at him. Should she tell him there were no such things? That fairies didn't exist? No, she told herself, let them enjoy it. They'll find out soon enough.

‘Well, I can’t really help you there, I’m afraid,’ she said. ‘Fairy rings are a thing of nature, they just appear.’

Fred gave a final swallow. ‘Oh, I know it’s coming,’ he said, with certainty. ‘But I’m just hoping it comes in time for Lucy’s birthday.’

‘You know it’s coming?’

‘Yup,’ he said. ‘But if it doesn’t, it might be because I used a button. Course, it was a really nice button and Mrs Pickles said it would probably be very useful. They’ll probably use it for a sieve or something, with all those holes in, or they could put a tiny twig in each hole and use it as a table.’

‘What an excellent idea,’ said Zinnia.

‘I got loads more,’ he said. ‘if you want to hear them.’

‘Well, I’d love to, but could you save them for next time? I’ve got to catch the bus. Bye-bye, Fred.’

‘Bye, Miss!’

‘*It’s come*! *We’ve got it*!’

Gerald Douglas glanced up as Fred landed with a crash against the fence.

‘Good morning, Fred,’ he said.

‘Hello, Mr Douglas. We’ve got it!’

Gerald was feeling at peace with the world that morning. He hadn’t managed to think of the final clue and his pride wouldn’t let him cheat, so he put it to one side and congratulated himself on completing the rest of it.

Now, he had a refreshing mug of tea in one hand, a delicious croissant in the other and the new crossword spread on the table in front of him. Life was sweet, and even Fred couldn't put a dent in his new-found happiness.

'So, what is it exactly that you've got?'

'Our fairy ring!' Fred cried. 'I ordered it, and it's come! *And* there's still two days to go before Lucy's birthday!'

Gerald took a sip of his tea. He knew you could get pretty much anything on the internet these days, but a fairy ring?

'A fairy ring? Where d'you get that then? Did your dad order it from a seed catalogue?'

Fred spluttered. 'You can't buy them,' he said. 'Miss Pickles says it's a thing of nature, so I ordered it from the fairies.'

Gerald took a bite of his croissant and chewed thoughtfully. Should he tell him there were no such things? That fairies didn't exist? No, he'll find out soon enough.

'I see,' he said. 'How much was it?'

'One button,' said Fred.

By this time, Gerald was beginning to wonder if a young man not a million miles away was having him on a piece of string. Another one of his jokes, presumably.

'I see,' he said. Rising from his chair, he walked across to the fence. Perhaps it was time to call Fred's bluff. 'I'd rather like to see this fairy ring,' he said, with a straight face. 'Can you show it to me?'

'Course! Look! Just there!'

Gerald looked down into Fred's garden. There, in a perfect little circle of six tiny toadstools, was a beautiful fairy ring. Gerald stared at it for a moment. That certainly wasn't a plastic replica, that was the real thing.

'Well,' he said, at last. 'You're right. That is a splendid fairy ring. Lucky old you.'

'I could ask the fairies if you'd like one,' Fred said. 'Next time I go to see Miss Pickles, I can ask. Have you got a button?'

'Um, Fred,' Gerald said. 'About fairies …'

Fred grinned. 'I *know*,' he said. 'Mrs Pickles told me. It's got to be real ones, not like the Cottingley ones, they weren't real.'

'The Cottingley Fairies? Oh yes, I remember reading about that. Mrs Pickles is quite right, they weren't -'

Gerald froze. 'Cottingley,' he murmured.

'Yup,' said Fred.

'Fred! You're a genius!'

'Well, I think I might be, 'cause I do think loads of genius stuff.'

'You certainly are, lad! It's the answer to the last clue!' Reaching across, Gerald ruffled Fred's hair. 'You clever boy!'

In their cosy sitting room, Zinnia replaced the phone on its receiver. The caller had been Grace, Fred's mum. Fred had made a terrible fuss about the fairy ring and wanted to tell her and Marigold all about it. Could she have a quick word with him?

Zinnia had been only too happy to chat to Fred about the marvellous fairy ring he was convinced was an order straight from the fairies. The *real* fairies, he added, because the Cottingley Fairies wouldn't have sent it, but could she say thank you to Mrs Pickles for telling him all about them, because it had given Mr Douglas the last clue.

Smiling, Zinnia walked across to the window and watched her mum tending the hanging baskets. Mum would be pleased to hear about Fred's fairy ring, and secretly, she would probably believe it was a gift from the fairies of Bluebell Copse.

Zinnia walked across to the drawer of the desk and lifted out a small box. A tiny photograph lay inside, wrapped in tissue paper. It was the photograph taken by her great-grandfather in Bluebell Copse all those years ago.

She unwrapped it for another look. Two little girls sitting in the sunshine on a large stone pot. She stared at it. Could that stone pot really have been only six inches high?

Looking down the garden, she watched her mum hang a basket in Bluebell Copse.

I wonder, she thought. I wonder.

Fred and The Penny Arcade

Nigel Stone slid a penny into the slot, flicked the handle, and watched as the metal ball whizzed around the hoops.

It was three years since he'd moved down to Castletop Bay, a quiet little seaside town off the beaten track. It was just the sort of resort he liked, old-fashioned and relatively untouched.

The Penny Arcade, tucked away in the arches, had been up for sale, and enchanted by the old penny slot machines of his childhood, Nigel had bought it there and then.

After a slow start, the business had been doing fairly well. It was never going to make him rich, but supplied a steady income, and everything was going swimmingly until Freddie's Fun Palace arrived. Loud, brash, full of flashing lights and even flashier machines, it occupied three arches between Cecil's Studio, and Gail's Gifts.

Nigel didn't begrudge the trade it brought the other businesses in the town, but couldn't help wishing it had set up on the south beach instead of the north.

The moment it opened, trade at The Penny Arcade plummeted, and Nigel was forced to consider whether this might have to be his last season.

'Hello, Mr Stone.'

Nigel turned to see a young boy in a luminous tee-shirt and shorts, flip-flopping his way towards him.

Fred Bunting.

Fred was staying with his family in The Barley Mow, a small pub and hotel, where he had wasted no time introducing himself to the staff and anyone else that would listen.

Nigel liked Fred, who'd been a regular customer at The Penny Arcade since his arrival.

'Hello there, Fred,' said Nigel. 'Good morning to you. Come to have another go on the racing?'

'Yes, please.'

Such a nice polite child, thought Nigel. A bright lad, too, and so refreshingly quiet.

Fred's subsequent shriek shattered his eardrums. 'LUCY! YOU HAVING A GO ON THE RACING?'

The deafening response from Fred's sister told Nigel that she would indeed like a go on the racing.

Shortly after, Lucy arrived with their mother, Grace, a small lady with lots of springy hair restrained with a large clip. She impressed Nigel as a calm woman who took everything in her stride, possibly the only way she kept her sanity.

'Good morning, Mr Stone.'

'Good morning to you, Mrs Bunting.'

Grace Bunting reached into her purse. 'Fifty pence worth of old pennies, please, Mr Stone. Now, dear,' she added, turning to Fred, who was gripping his little sister's hand whether she liked it or not, 'that's half each. You show Lucy how to play the racing game. And remember, anything she wins stays in her tray. Ok?'

Fred nodded, eyes wide as Nigel counted the large brown pennies into his hand.

Nigel never tired of the effect old pennies had on the children. They were so much more substantial than the new money. It looked a huge amount, even if it wasn't.

'Thanks, Mr Stone! C'mon Lucy!'

'Fred?'

Fred turned.

'I'll be right here,' said his mum. She pointed to a small collection of old-fashioned metal buckets, that Nigel kept as a side-line. They were a little more expensive, but sturdy.

'I'd better have two of these buckets,' she said. 'Perhaps this will last him a little longer. His first bucket met its doom yesterday when he was conducting one of his scientific experiments with wave power. It's better known as leaving your bucket a little too near the incoming tide.'

Nigel laughed. 'He's a bright lad.'

Grace gazed at Fred, proudly. 'He certainly is.'

Nigel was a little earlier than usual when he arrived back at The Barley Mow.

The Barley Mow was an old building, with eight bedrooms, one of which was a family room currently occupied by the Buntings. Set in large grounds at the very end of the High Street, The Barley Mow could have been lifted from a jigsaw box. An elderly rose rambled around the doorway and tables with brightly coloured umbrellas dotted the front patio.

Nigel had a lovely room overlooking the meadow and in return for his bed and board, he did any odd jobs and took care of the garden for Briony Hope, the owner. It was an arrangement that suited them both.

Briony looked up as Nigel walked into reception. 'Hello Nigel, love, how was business today?'

Nigel shrugged. 'Slow,' he said. 'Think I might have to call it a day.'

'Oh, what a shame.'

'Oh well. It is what it is. I'll see how things go.'

'Course.' She looked at him. 'I've made a nice steak pie for dinner tonight.'

'I love steak pie,' yelled a voice.

Fred came running down the stairs. 'I love steak pie,' he said. 'Course, my mum's pies are the best in the world, especially her steak and kidney. They've won loads of prizes, and last time, at the Fair -'

'Thank you, Fred, that'll do.' Grace Bunting's cheeks were a little pink. She turned to Briony. 'I'm so sorry,' she said. 'I can't tell you how lovely it's been not to have to do the cooking. You're a wonderful cook.'

'A compliment indeed,' said Briony. She winked at Grace. 'From the World Champion.'

Grace shook her head. 'Oh dear, he means well.'

‘Thought I might nip back early and make a start on sorting that outbuilding for you, Briony,’ Nigel said.

‘Is there going to be treasure?’ Fred asked, his mouth half-open.

‘Fred! Come along,’ said Grace. ‘It’s rude to listen to other people’s conversations.’

‘How am I supposed to know anything, then?’

Grace shook her head.

‘That would be wonderful,’ said Briony, laughing as she watched them go. ‘Thanks, Nigel. I’ve been meaning to do it for ages. Nothing to do with the spiders, of course.’

Nigel chuckled. ‘Course not,’ he said. ‘Don’t worry, I’ll get my safari gear on.’

Walking up to his room to change, Nigel thought about the old building in the field beside the hotel. He’d have a good look at the condition of it while he was in there. He wasn’t sure what plans Briony had for it, but his knowledge and experience as a surveyor might come in useful.

Ten minutes later, he was standing before the open doors of the outbuilding, astonished. He knew Briony used it for storage. He knew, also, that she was a keen visitor to boot sales, garden fairs and auctions, but he had no idea she’d amassed so much.

‘Oh, my goodness,’ he said. ‘This is going to be a job and a half.’

‘I could do the half,’ said a voice behind him.

Nigel turned to see Fred, now wearing jeans, a lurid tee-shirt and a baseball cap back to front.

‘Oh, hello again, Fred, what are you up to?’

Fred launched into an explanation. 'Mum says I can play in the garden while Lucy has a nap, but I'm too old for playing, so I thought I might help you or Miss Hope. I did ask Miss Hope, but she says I'm not allowed in the kitchen so I'll have to help you.'

'I see.'

He looked up to see Grace Bunting at an upstairs window. 'I hope you're not making a nuisance of yourself.'

'I'm going to help Mr Stone,' Fred called. 'We're going to look for stuff.'

Grace Bunting gave Nigel a look that asked, 'Is that ok?'

He replied with a gentle nod. 'Right,' he said. 'We'd best get on.'

After an hour of lifting, sorting, cobwebs and spiders, enough of the contents were outside on the grass to enable Nigel to get a good look at the building, inside and out.

'Well,' he said, 'it looks like it's still sound. For an old building.'

'We're doing about old buildings at school,' Fred said. 'Castles 'n' that. The biggest castle in England is Windsor Castle, where the King sometimes lives when he's not living somewhere else.'

'Indeed it is.'

'And,' said Fred, 'they were made from wood first off, but then they made them from stone, so people couldn't get in and they all wore garden robes.'

'Garden robes?'

'Yup. Probably for doing the garden. And the first castles were made by Mr Mott and Mr Bailey, who were really good builders.'

Nigel took a breath, while he considered. Was it worth the risk of a very long conversation if he explained about motte and bailey castles? More to the point, would it even be a good idea to explain about a garderobe?

'My goodness,' he cried. 'Look at the size of that spider.'

To his relief, Fred dashed off to have a look, but was back in under a minute, hands cupped.

'I've got him, Mr Stone! Look at the size of him! He's massive!'

Spiders had never been a problem for Nigel. A lifelong nature lover, he couldn't bring himself to hurt any living thing, but when Fred opened his hands to reveal the Arnold Schwarzenegger of the spider world, Nigel felt a chill run up his spine.

'That, um … yes, that certainly is a cracker,' he said, edging away.

'D'you want to hold it?'

Nigel looked down at Arnie, sitting in Fred's palm, flexing his many muscular legs.

'Er, no thanks, Fred. And you mustn't keep hold of it either, it's not good for them. Go and release it over there.' He looked up to see Briony approaching with two drinks on a tray.

'How's it going?' she asked. 'Any luck?'

'We've found loads of stuff,' said Fred. 'And a ginormous spider.' He opened his hands.

Briony took a quick step backwards. ‘How exciting.’

‘Go and release it, there’s a good lad.’ Nigel took a glass of lemonade. ‘Thank you, Briony. D’you know, you have a lot of very good things here. The retro things are probably quite valuable. And the signs, and the furniture. You’ve got some museum pieces here I shouldn’t wonder.’

‘Well, it’s only local stuff,’ she said. ‘But I like things with a bit of social history to them. I was thinking of maybe opening a small museum, for the village, you know. What d’you reckon? Silly idea?’

‘That’s a brilliant idea!’ said Fred, returning. ‘That’s a brilliant idea, isn’t it, Mr Stone?’

‘I rather think it is,’ said Nigel.

‘It can be like the olden days. And you can put your machines in it.’

‘My machines, Fred?’

‘Your penny machines. They’re really old. You can move them here, and then when we come down on holiday, I can play with them and I won’t have to go down to the beach! Course, you’ll have to get some ice creams as well, ‘cause me and Lucy like ice cream. Otherwise, it’ll all melt by the time we get back.’

‘I’ll make sure I have a few ice creams in the freezer for you both,’ said Briony. ‘Now, off you go, your mum wants you.’

Sitting together for a moment, Briony and Nigel watched as Fred ran indoors.

‘What do you think of his idea?’ Briony said, casually. ‘You know, about moving your machines here. It would save you the expense at the arches, and they could be part of the museum.'

Nigel thought for a moment. 'I suppose it is an idea. You wouldn't mind? I'd pay rent, of course.'

'Don't be daft,' she said. 'I wouldn't hear of it. You'd be doing me a favour.'

Nigel looked at her. 'Right, well, I'll get the museum sorted, and move them in, shall I?'

Briony put a hand on his arm. 'Lovely,' she said.

'Fred!'

Fred turned.

Dipping into her apron, Briony gave him a shiny pound coin. 'Thank you for mentioning about the machines,' she said. 'It's the obvious solution, but I couldn't think how to broach the subject without hurting his feelings.'

'Thanks, Miss Hope!'

'Ah, good morning, Fred,' said Nigel, as they walked into The Penny Arcade. 'Come for another go on the racing? No, please, these are on me,' he said, as Grace reached for her purse. 'Fred was very helpful yesterday.'

'That's kind of you.'

'My pleasure.' Nigel watched as Fred headed for the racing game. 'Psst! Fred!'

Fred walked back. 'Thanks for yesterday,' he whispered. 'I've thought for a while that building would be ideal for the machines, but it would have been a terrible imposition to ask. Here -'

He passed him a shiny pound coin. 'Get yourself an ice-cream.'

'Thanks, Mr Stone!'

Slipping the coin into his pocket, Fred put two old pennies on Purple Lady to win.

Fred and Ginger

'Hello, Miss Trumble.'

Olivia Trumble looked up from her gardening. Leaning over the garden gate was a small boy.

Fred Bunting lived three doors away in their quiet little street and often stopped for a chat when he was out on his bike.

'Hello, there, Fred,' she said. 'How are you?'

'I'm fine, thank you. What are you doing?'

'Just getting rid of these weeds,' she said. 'And I'm also trying to decide what to call my new cat.'

'Wow! Have you got a new cat, Miss? Where is he?'

'It's a she,' said Olivia. 'She isn't here yet. I'm picking her up this afternoon.'

Fred leaned a little further over the gate. 'Did you get her from Mrs Cuthbert? Mrs Cuthbert's got loads of kittens.'

'Well, actually, I didn't, I wanted to give an adult cat a home, you see, and Mrs Cuthbert only has kittens at the moment, so I popped up to Top Hat

Animal Rescue. It's a lovely place out in the country and they look after lots of animals while they wait for new homes.'

'Oh,' said Fred. 'Well, old cats are nice, too. My Grandad's got a cat called Reg and he's twenty.'

Olivia nodded. She'd heard about Reg, most of the village had. Reg was 'retired' now, but in his youth he'd roamed the village like a small gangster.

'That's a wonderful age,' she said.

'Grandad says it's because they don't do much.'

'Perhaps they do more than we think. I saw a programme once where they fitted little cameras to their collars. Some cats go ever such a long way.'

Fred shook his head. 'Reg doesn't,' he said. 'He used to go a long way years ago, and sometimes he was gone for days. Nan said sometimes Grandad wished he'd go even further, 'cause he used to dig up the flowerbeds, but now he doesn't do much at all.'

Olivia smiled. 'Well, twenty is well over a hundred in our years, Fred. I guess he's earned a rest at his age. I expect he thinks a lot. They're very intelligent creatures, you know.'

Fred was quiet for a moment, then he asked, 'Why don't cats have wrinkles?'

Olivia put down her fork and looked at him. 'D'you know, that's a very good question, I've never thought about it. Perhaps they do, but they're under their fur.'

'I'm going to have a look when we go to Grandad's later,' he said. 'See if Reg has got any wrinkles.'

'I see,' she said. 'Well, be careful not to disturb him when you look. He might not like it.'

'Reg won't mind,' Fred said, confidently. 'Cats like me. It's just natural.'

'That's because you respect them,' she said, pulling off her gloves. 'And you're kind and loving.'

'And it's probably 'cause I give them treats. I'll let you know if I find any wrinkles. Bye!'

Olivia chuckled to herself as Fred rode away. It was a mild, quiet day, but she still felt slightly windswept.

It was almost two o'clock, and Olivia was sitting in the chair watching her beautiful new tortoiseshell cat, Ginger.

'After Ginger Rogers,' she told herself, watching as the slender cat tripped the light fantastic with a cotton reel. 'She's so graceful and nimble.'

Ginger had jumped straight onto her lap that afternoon and Olivia was overjoyed. It had only been a couple of days and she seemed such a sweet, docile little cat.

Fred had already visited with his mum and sister Lucy, and, like every other animal, Ginger had rushed to Fred, purring and warbling, curling around his legs like a snake. It was known in the village as The Fred Effect.

The doorbell rang.

'Oh, there's the bell, sweetheart,' she said to Ginger, who had just resettled on her lap. 'I'm sorry, I'll have to move you.'

Ginger's immediate reaction was to sink in her claws. Fortunately, Olivia had thought to put a cushion beneath and moved her gently onto the chair without injury.

'Yowl!' said Ginger.

'I'll be back,' she said. 'You have a nice rest.'

On the doorstep stood her neighbour, Vernon Partridge. It was two years since Olivia had moved to the village and when Vernon called to introduce himself, they'd hit it off straight away.

'Morning, Vernon. Fancy a cup of coffee?'

'I'd love one,' he said, stepping into the hallway. He looked vaguely in the direction of the sitting room. 'Fred tells me your new cat is receiving visitors. Ok to have a peek?'

'Of course. She loves visitors.'

They went through into the sitting room. Ginger had left the cushion and was now stretched out on the sofa like a Hollywood diva at rest. As they walked in, she looked up and gave Vernon a thirty-second appraisal. Her tail started to flick.

'D'you think that's a good sign?'

Olivia shrugged. 'Bit early to say. Best take it slow.'

Taking tentative steps, Vernon looked everywhere but at Ginger and rested a hand on the back of the settee.

A low growl rumbled in Ginger's throat.

'Oh,' said Olivia.

'She's bound to be nervous,' Vernon said, with a courageous chuckle. 'She's never met me before. Torties are often timid.'

He moved his arm slowly along the settee. 'You're lovely, aren't you, sweetheart?'

Ginger hissed like a deflating balloon. Her paw flew out, claws primed and newly sharpened.

Vernon pulled his hand swiftly out of reach. 'Maybe … um … maybe I should give it a while,' he said. 'Try again another time.'

'Maybe,' Olivia said. She was devastated. She hadn't mentioned it to anyone else, but she'd become rather fond of Vernon. He was a nice, kind soul, who loved animals as she did, and she was so hoping Ginger would take to him. 'Everything's a bit new for her, I expect,' she said. 'Come and have some coffee.'

They adjourned to the kitchen.

'I named her after Ginger Rogers,' Olivia said, passing the biscuits. 'She's so lithe and graceful.'

'Y-e-s,' said Vernon, retreating nervously as Ginger walked into the kitchen and disappeared through the cat flap.

'I'm sure she'll be fine next time.'

Vernon accepted another biscuit. 'I do hope so,' he said, wistfully.

'She still isn't back,' said Olivia. She was standing on Vernon's doorstep, wringing her hands. It was almost three o'clock, and Ginger had been gone for some time.

'I'm probably being silly,' she said. 'But she usually comes straight back after … well, you know.'

Vernon hurried to slip on his shoes. 'Don't you worry, Liv, I'll come and help you look. I'm sure she's fine. Probably just finding her way about.'

They knocked at every door in the street and asked in the High Street shops.

'She's very pretty,' said Olivia, showing a photo.

Everyone agreed she was indeed very pretty and there was much oohing and aahing, but no one had seen her.

'She's lost,' Olivia said, sadly, as they walked home. 'I've only had her a few days and she's lost. I feel so guilty. I shouldn't have let her out.'

'Now don't go blaming yourself,' Vernon said, gently. 'She's probably sitting on the sofa as we speak.'

She wasn't. They searched the garden yet again and every room in the house, yet again, but there was no sign of her.

'Oh dear,' said Olivia. Tears welled in her eyes.

Vernon wrapped his arms around her. It was something he'd longed to do, but his courage had always deserted him. 'She'll be back,' he said, reassuringly. 'Now, you sit there and I'll make …'

Olivia's mobile phone suddenly rang. 'Yes?'

As Vernon watched, a smile lit up her face.

'She's safe!' she cried. 'She's bringing her home!'

'Who?'

'Fred's mum.' She laughed. 'You'll never guess. They found Ginger in the back of the car when they got to Fred's Grandad. Grace thinks she must've jumped in when she was loading the car. Isn't it wonderful!'

Without thinking, she threw her arms around Vernon's neck, and kissed him.

'Oh,' she said, moving away, her face flushed. 'Forgive me, I'm so sorry.'

Vernon smiled at her. With trembling hands, he pulled her gently back into his arms. 'Don't be,' he whispered.

'And *then*,' said Fred, pausing for breath, 'there she was, curled on a cushion Mum was taking over for Reg. It's Reg's favourite cushion with all birds on it, and he used to use it when he walked to us, but he doesn't now because he's too old, so Mum thought he might like it now he's poorly as well as old.'

They were sitting in the living room. Olivia was serving tea and in a blur of undiluted happiness, Vernon was cutting cake.

On his return, Fred had walked down at once, Ginger following devotedly behind. As Olivia opened the door, Ginger had rushed to meet her, purring contentedly, and then, to Olivia's delight, strolled across to Vernon and wiped her nose on his leg. Not much, but it was a start.

'Maybe she likes you, after all,' she said, sipping her tea. She turned to Fred. 'Ginger didn't seem to take to Vernon at first, but it looks as though it's going to be ok.'

Fred looked down at Ginger, now stretched out on his lap. 'Mr Partridge is really nice, Ginger,' he said. He leaned a bit closer to whisper. 'You can't not like Mr Partridge, because he and Miss Trumble are in love.'

Olivia felt her face flush with heat. Beside her, Vernon's cake went down in a lump.

'Um …'

Vernon looked adoringly at the woman of his dreams, and took a deep breath. 'Yes,' he said, boldly. 'Yes, that's right. I love you, Olivia.'

'Told you,' said Fred.

'Yowl,' said Ginger.

'Oh, Vernon,' said Olivia. 'I love you, too.'

'Thank you, Fred, for all your help with finding Ginger,' Olivia said, later.

Standing beside her, Vernon reached into his pocket and pulled out a shiny pound coin. 'There you go, Fred,' he said. 'Get yourself some sweets. You're a good lad.'

'Thanks, Mr Partridge! Bye! Bye, Ginger!'

'Yowl!' said Ginger, perched on the garden fence.

Fred took a few steps, then turned. 'Miss Trumble,' he said, 'why did you call her Ginger? She's only a bit ginger.'

'After Ginger Rogers,' said Olivia. 'She's very graceful, just like she was.'

'Who's Ginger Rogers?'

'She was a famous dancer,' said Vernon, hoping it wasn't the start of one of Fred's long conversations. 'She often danced with Fred Astaire.'

Fred's eyes lit up at the mention of a famous Fred. 'Who was he?'

'He was also a dancer,' said Olivia. 'Very famous. He was a superb tap-dancer and Ginger Rogers used to match him step for step. Except of course, she did a lot of it backwards.'

'Why?'

Vernon's heart sank. Why, oh why, had he mentioned Fred Astaire?

'I've got a great idea,' said Olivia, hastily. 'How about you come around another day and we'll watch one of their films. It's called Top Hat and you'll see how, and why, Ginger Rogers dances backwards, ok?'

'And there's another film called Royal Wedding,' said Vernon, getting carried away, 'where Fred dances on the ceiling …'

Too late, he realised his mistake. Fred's mouth had dropped open.

'And we'll watch that one, too,' said Olivia, quickly. 'Bye for now, Fred.'

Sitting beside Ginger in the garden the following week, Fred stroked her head.

'Top Hat was brilliant,' he said. 'Fred Astaire danced the piccalilli with Ginger Rogers and they never fell over once.' He looked down at Ginger. 'You're going to be happy here, Ginge. Miss Trumble's very kind, and I bet you'll get loads of fish 'n' stuff, if you ask.'

Ginger gazed at him with eyes of love.

'Just one thing,' Fred continued. 'Don't go catching any birds, 'cause Mr Partridge likes them. He did a talk last year about Lesser Spotted Woodpeckers and it was really boring, but I didn't tell him, 'cause that's manners.'

A stray gust of wind blew a pine cone in their direction. Ginger leaped to her feet and did a balletic dance, pirouetting, and throwing it into the air.

'Wow!' said Fred. 'You're a brilliant dancer, and you can dance backwards, just like Ginger Rogers!'

Fred and The Pink Lady

'Miss Bell?'

The words interrupted a rare moment of peace in the busy classroom, and Ursula Bell allowed herself the luxury of a two-second pause before she looked up from her desk.

She already knew whose hand would be in the air, waiting patiently for a response. There was no mistaking it, Fred Bunting asked almost as many questions as Morrison Murray, quizmaster at The Three Crowns.

When Ursula offered to step in as supply teacher, Adelaide Flowers had thought it best to mention Fred Bunting, who was a bright, inquisitive boy, inclined to ask rather a lot of questions. Ursula had quickly reassured her. It wouldn't be a problem, she said, she'd taught children like Fred before. He was obviously one of those little loves who had an intelligence and curiosity beyond their years.

Now it was almost two o'clock on the first day and Ursula was beginning to realise exactly what Adelaide had meant.

Trying not to sigh, she looked up. 'Yes, Fred?'

Please, she thought, let it be something sensible this time. History was quite demanding enough without Fred rewriting it.

'Why didn't King Harold wear safety glasses?' Fred asked. 'Only if he did, he wouldn't have got hurt by the arrow. My dad wears safety glasses all the time and he hasn't been hurt by an arrow. Course, he did hit his thumb once and …'

'My dad wears safety glasses,' Ben said, from a desk nearby.

'And mine,' said Amelia.

'Bet your mum doesn't wear them,' Sophie said. 'My mum does. She does carpentry 'n' that and dad says he's going to borrow her hammer next time he makes pastry 'cause it goes hard.'

'King Harold could've worn Ray-Burns,' Henry piped up.

'My sister's got Ray-Burns,' said Cecily.

'Now, now, that's enough.' Miss Bell held up a hand. 'Everyone quiet and sit up straight.'

There was much scraping and dragging of chairs.

'Now,' she said. 'No more questions. You need to finish your designs for the village tapestry. There's all the stitching still to be done.'

'I'm going to be brilliant at stitches!' Fred said.

Quite likely, Ursula thought, as an industrious peace settled once more on the classroom.

She chuckled to herself. Fred probably would have an aptitude for stitches. From everything she'd heard, he had half the village in stitches at times.

The Little Mopham Tapestry was the brainchild of Humphrey Egg. An amateur historian, Humphrey had been delighted to discover that this year marked an important anniversary and his idea of a tapestry to tell the history of the village was immediately popular.

Everyone had been asked to contribute and the members of The Little Mopham Craft Society had volunteered to stitch all the panels together to make a beautiful tapestry for the Village Hall.

'I think we can all agree it's a tremendous idea,' the Mayoress said, as she announced the plans. 'I'm sure we'd all like to say a big thank you to Mr Humphrey Egg.'

She waved a hand toward Humphrey, seated in the front row. A round of applause rippled through the hall.

Humphrey Egg beamed. At that moment, it felt as though life couldn't get any better. The village had been delighted with his idea, he was in charge of research for the panels and now, to top it all, he was sitting in the village hall next to the woman he adored.

'Well done, Humphrey,' Ursula said.

He turned to her and felt his heart swell. 'Thank you.'

'There will also be a parade and a carnival,' the Mayoress continued. 'Applications and ideas for floats by the end of the month, please.'

‘I’ve got an idea and it’s brilliant!’ said a voice.

Everyone turned to look at Fred Bunting, whose hand was in the air once again.

‘Not now, dear,’ his mother said, quickly. ‘We’ll talk about it when we get home. Here, have a toffee.’

Fred looked crestfallen, but accepted the toffee.

Moved by the look on Fred’s face and a strong belief that children were clear, concise thinkers who should be listened to, Humphrey stood up. Here, he thought, was an ideal opportunity to impress Ursula.

‘That’s quite all right, Mrs Bunting,’ he said. ‘Out of the mouths of babes, you know. If the Mayoress has no objection, perhaps Fred can share his idea with us?’

The hall was suddenly silent. Humphrey Egg was a relative newcomer to the village and the crowd bubbled as they waited for the inevitable. On the stage, Mayoress Carmichael raised an eyebrow. Sitting beside Humphrey, Ursula held her breath and waited.

‘Here is my idea,’ Fred began, grandly, getting to his feet. ‘One of them floats should be about Kings and Queens.’

‘Kings and Queens, Fred?’

‘Yup,’ said Fred. ‘Kings and Queens. There’s been lots of them since years ago when the village opened, and we could have them all sitting on their thrones on a float and they could wave as they go by. It would be brilliant if the real King could come, ‘cause he could show them how to wave properly, but he might be too busy, so maybe we could ask someone else famous.’

Humphrey's eyes opened wide. 'Someone famous? To open the carnival, you mean? Now that *is* a brilliant idea.'

Fred slipped the toffee casually from one side of his mouth to the other. 'Told you,' he slurped. '*And* we can have King Harold and William the Conker. My Grandad says …'

'That's enough now, Fred.' John Bunting slipped a restraining arm about his son's shoulder.

'Someone famous?' Humphrey muttered, as the villagers filed out of the hall.

'A celebrity?' Ursula breathed. 'That would put Little Mopham on the map, wouldn't it, Humphrey? But who could we ask? I don't know anyone.'

'No problem,' he said, recklessly. 'Leave this to me. I know one or two people.'

Ursula gazed at him, with a look that melted his heart.

Please say she loves me, thought Humphrey.

Later that afternoon on a seat by the duck pond, Humphrey stared dolefully down at the brown earth. The sun was shining and a duck had mistaken his toe for a piece of bread, but he barely noticed.

He'd been walking through the village when he realised. He *knew* one or two people? What on earth had made him say that? He didn't know anyone famous and now he'd have to let her down.

'Want a bite of my apple?'

Slowly, he looked up. Fred was standing beside him. 'No thank you, Fred.'

'It's a pink lady.'

‘Who is?’

‘My apple,’ said Fred. ‘It’s a pink lady.’

‘Oh.’

Ursula looked lovely in pink, Humphrey thought to himself. It went so well with her beautiful hair.

‘What you doing?’

Humphrey sighed. ‘Thinking.’

‘I’m brilliant at thinking.’

‘I know you are.’

‘And ideas. I’m brilliant at them, too.’

‘You certainly are. That was a wonderful idea you had this morning, only ...’

Fred bit his apple and chewed slowly. ‘Only what?’

‘Well, we need to find a celebrity and I don’t know anyone. Anyone famous, I mean. I told Miss Bell I knew one or two people but I don’t.’

‘Miss Bell won’t mind. She’s really nice.’

‘I know she is.’ He turned to see Fred staring at him.

‘Are you and Miss Bell in love, Mr Egg?’

Humphrey paused. Kids have clear, concise minds, he told himself, no point in trying to conceal things. ‘Well … well, as it happens, I am in love with Miss Bell.’

‘I thought you was.’

‘Did you? Oh heavens, is it that obvious?’

‘Course. Your eyes was going all funny.’

Humphrey’s heart skipped a beat. ‘Were Miss Bell’s eyes going ‘all funny’ as well?’

‘No,’ said Fred. He looked up. ‘Coming Mum! You leave it to me, Mr Egg. I’m brilliant at problems.

I s'pect the answer's ten, anyway, ten's the answer to loads of things. Got to go now. Bye!'

'Bye-bye, Fred.'

Dejectedly, Humphrey began the long walk home. A celebrity? What on earth was he going to do?

'Mr Egg! Mr Egg!'

Humphrey put down a plant. 'Hello there, Fred! What are you up to?'

'I'm here with Dad. We always come to the market on Sunday. What you doing?'

'I'm just looking at these plants.'

'Are you going to buy one for Miss Bell?'

Humphrey paused. He was beginning to wish he hadn't confided in Fred. 'Possibly.'

'Is it for her birthday?'

'Her birthday?'

'Yup. It's the day of the carnival,' Fred said, airily. 'She told us. And she's bringing in a cake to school. I s'pect it'll be a big one with chocolate on and buttons 'n' that so we can all have some.'

'Well that's kind.'

'Yup. *And*,' he said, leaning closer. 'I've found one.'

'What have you found?'

'A celeriac to open the carnival.'

'You mean a celebrity?'

'That's what I said. It's Mrs Appleby. She's 103 and she lives in Chestnut Lodge. Mum says she's had cards from the Queen so she must be famous.'

Humphrey felt his spirits rise. 'Fred,' he said. 'That is an excellent idea.'

Two weeks later the village of Little Mopham woke up to a gloriously sunny Carnival Day.

At precisely two o'clock a delighted Mrs Appleby, elegantly attired in pink, arrived to open the carnival and admire the wonderful tapestry soon to be hung in the village hall.

Our wonderful pink lady, Humphrey thought to himself. Well done, Fred.

All the local groups had decorated a float. Shopkeepers advertised and gave away samples and societies put on wonderful historic displays, while the local brass band and choral groups filled the air with music. In the field, dancers danced and pets performed in the hope of winning a prize.

Stalls selling a range of local products were doing a brisk trade and at the cheese stall Humphrey Egg was selecting one or two favourites.

'For after dinner,' he said to Ursula. 'I wondered, as it's your birthday, if you'd allow me to cook you dinner this evening?'

Ursula glanced at him. 'That's a coincidence. I was going to ask if you could join me for dinner this evening. It's not my birthday, it's yours … isn't it?'

Humphrey shook his head. 'Mine's in December.'

'So's mine, but Fred said ...'

They stared at each other for a moment, then started to laugh.

'Perhaps he was hoping for two cakes,' she said. 'Yes, thank you, Humphrey, I'd love to.'

Thank you, Fred, Humphrey thought, as his heart threatened to burst. I've always said children should be listened to. Although …

Turning, he slipped his hand into Ursula's. 'What say we go and find our young friend and treat him to a nice cake to say thank you?'

'I think that's a wonderful idea,' she said, smiling. 'I could do with a cup of tea.'

'Fred?'

Fred looked up.

'We wondered if you'd like a hot doughnut,' said Ursula. She offered a bag.

'Wow! Thanks, Miss.'

'And I wanted to say thank you, too,' said Humphrey.

Fred stopped eating. 'But you haven't got a doughnut.'

'No.' Humphrey shook his head. 'No, I mean for your advice. You know, about a celeriac … I mean celebrity. You saved my bacon.'

Fred looked alarmed. 'But Mr Egg, I didn't save you any bacon. Mum made bacon sandwiches this morning, but …'

'No, sorry, what I meant was you helped me with my problem. Although,' he added, with a smile, 'ten wasn't the answer to this one, was it?'

'It was.'

Humphrey frowned. 'How?'

Fred wiped the sugar from his mouth. 'Mrs Appleby's flat in Chestnut Lodge is number ten,' he said. 'Which is brilliant, isn't it?'

Fred's Birthday

'Um …'

Grace Bunting looked at her son. 'Fred, you're the first child I've ever known who doesn't know what he wants for his birthday.'

Fred's eyes opened wide with indignation. 'I *do*,' he said. 'I want loads of stuff. Can I have loads of stuff?'

Grace shook her head. 'I don't think so. You can have one thing, and there'll be one or two surprises, as usual. Now, have a think and let me know. Ok?'

'Ok, Mum. Can I have a party?'

Grace closed her eyes. She'd known this question was coming. The very fact that Fred had mentioned it several weeks before, meant it was coming. Fred was a bright boy, who soaked up knowledge like a sponge, and once mentioned, things were not forgotten.

'We'll see,' she said. 'Have a think about your present.'

Sliding a sandwich into Fred's lunchbox, Grace snapped the lid shut. A party? She'd better have a think.

'It's my birthday next Saturday,' said Fred, cheerfully. 'And I'm having a party. D'you want to come?'

Dozing contentedly beneath his newspaper, Gerald Douglas switched on his deaf ear. It was a useful facility when one lived next door to Fred Bunting.

In truth, he was fond of Fred. They had a great many interesting conversations, but unfortunately, Fred had been born without an Off switch. Most days this wasn't a problem and Gerald was happy to answer his questions, but today wasn't one of those days.

It began with the toe-stubbing, an incident that had robbed Gerald of coherent speech for a full two minutes. In a fit of rage, he had kicked the offending bed-leg with his other foot and was now nursing two badly bruised toes.

Shortly after, he'd knocked his tea over his crisp, clean morning newspaper, before he could even glance at the crossword.

Gerald stepped outside to lay out the paper to dry, and then, in a flash of inspiration, decided it would dry all the quicker across his face as he sat in the deckchair.

He was just dozing beautifully, when Fred's question shattered his eardrums.

A silent groan bubbled in Gerald's throat. Oh, no. Keep quiet, he told himself. Keep quiet and he'll go away.

'Mr Douglas!'

Gerald gave an exaggerated snore.

'Mr *Douglas*!'

Carefully pushing aside the newspaper, Gerald stared at him, blearily. 'You shrieked?'

Fred's eyes opened wide. 'Sorry, Mr Douglas, was you asleep? It's very early. I don't go to bed till seven.'

'Goodness me, no, I wasn't asleep,' said Gerald. 'I was making sure my eyelids still worked.'

'That's brilliant! I'm going to try that.'

For the next minute or so, Gerald watched in amazement as the small boy draped over the garden fence gave his eyelids a workout.

'I should stop now, Fred,' he said. 'You'll make your eyes ache.'

'Ok. D'you want to come to my birthday party, Mr Douglas? Mum says I can have one if I want.'

Gerald hesitated, while he racked his brains for an excuse. 'Well,' he began. 'It's very nice of you to invite me …'

'Brilliant! I'm going to write a list of who's coming and you're going to be the first. Bye, Mr Douglas!'

Gerald's head dropped forward. He'd done it again.

Blotting out the world once more with his newspaper, he closed his eyes. What on earth could he get Fred for a present? He'd better have a think.

'Hello, Mr Meredith!'

Colin Meredith looked up. 'Ah,' he said. 'Hello, Fred. Come to see Ben and Molly? They're indoors. Go on in.'

'Thank you,' said Fred. 'I've got something special to ask them.'

'Really? That sounds interesting.'

'Yup. It's my birthday soon and I'm having a party. Can Ben and Molly come?'

'Oh, I think they probably will,' he said, knowing wild horses wouldn't keep them away. 'That's very nice of you.'

'And you,' said Fred. 'And Mrs Meredith. You're all invited.'

Visions of a nice, quiet few hours in the garden with Margaret while the twins were out, faded slowly. 'Oh, you don't want us old 'uns there,' Colin said, desperately. 'You kids can have more fun.'

Fred looked down at Bob, the Merediths' dog, who had hurtled down the path at the sound of his voice, and was now glued to his leg.

'Hello, Bob!' he said, bending down to stroke him. Colin watched as Bob melted into a pool of fur.

'Bob can come, too,' said Fred. 'Bye, Mr Meredith!'

Watching Fred go in through the back gate with Bob, Colin picked up his coffee and continued on his way to his little workshop in the garden. It was his haven, his little escape from the world. In his workshop Colin worked on the things that would have made him a fortune if someone else hadn't beaten him to it.

Thoughtfully, Colin picked up his pencil and slid it behind his ear. Maybe he could make Fred something for his birthday? He'd have a bit of a think.

'Want to come to my party?'

Olivia Trumble was pegging out the last of her washing. It was a lovely windy day and she scarcely heard Fred's call across four garden fences.

'Someone's calling you,' said Vernon Partridge, holding the basket for her. It was a simple, everyday task, but to Vernon, everyday task plus time spent with the love of his life equalled heaven. Unbeknown to Olivia, his proposal plans were in full swing.

Olivia looked around. 'Hello there Fred,' she called. 'Are you ok?'

'Yes, thank you. Want to come to my party?'

Olivia leaned on the washing line. 'A party?'

'Yup. It's my birthday next Saturday and I'm having a party and you can both come if you want. Everyone's coming!'

Olivia looked at Vernon. 'We can make that, can't we?'

Vernon gripped the sides of the washing basket as though his life depended on it. 'Would that be next Saturday?'

Olivia turned back to the fence. 'Did you say next Saturday, dear?'

'Yup,' said Fred. 'There'll be loads of food and balloons and stuff.'

‘Oh, sounds wonderful!’ called Olivia, delightedly. ‘We’ll be there!’

Turning back to Vernon, she whispered, ‘He’s such a dear boy, isn’t he? We can’t disappoint him. Is that okay for you, love?’

‘Yes,’ said Vernon, monotonously, rearranging next Saturday’s planned proposal in his mind.

Olivia turned on her heels. ‘Let’s go and have a coffee and see what we can come up with.’

‘Come up with?’

‘For his present,’ she said. ‘We’ll need to have a bit of a think.’

Hilda Dunbar picked up the little fairy cottage she’d tucked away in the crook of a tree. It was definitely in need of a coat of paint. Just a garden ornament, of course, but one never knew. No self-respecting fairy would want a tatty home.

Of course, she’d never breathe a word about things like that to anyone else. No one except Gordon, that is, but he was different. Gordon was in tune with the environment, and sensitive to the world around him, as she was. He never dismissed things out of hand and always kept an open mind. So important, Hilda told herself, when there’s so much about this world of ours we have yet to learn.

At a loud ringing noise, she glanced up. Fred Bunting was zooming down the street on his bicycle, repeatedly sounding his bell.

‘Is there a fire, Fred?’ Hilda asked, as he screeched to a halt.

'No,' he puffed. 'But I've got news, and in the olden days, they used to ring bells when there was news and they had special men called town fryers, who rang bells and shouted about it.'

'I think you mean town criers,' Hilda said, gently. 'Yes, they did do that. Especially if it was very important news.'

'Mine's very important news,' said Fred, grandly. 'It's my birthday next Saturday and I'm having a party and everyone's invited. There'll be loads of food and balloons and probably crackers, and other stuff.'

'Well, that does sound exciting,' said Hilda.

'You and Mr Pugh can come, too,' said Fred, generously.

'Oh, I see. Well, that is kind of you, Fred. I'll ask him.'

'He'll want to come all right. He likes parties, he told me.'

'I'm sure he will, Fred, but he may have other plans. He belongs to one or two clubs and things and sometimes he's busy on a Saturday.'

'Wow! Are they secret clubs, Miss Dunbar?'

'Oh no. Just model railways and gardening. He likes philately, too. Gordon's collected stamps since he was a child.'

Fred stared. 'What do they do with them?'

'Well … they look at them,' she said. 'And swap them, and things. Some are very valuable.'

'Are they worth millions and millions?'

'I believe some are,' she said. 'But of course, they're very rare.'

Fred gasped. 'I have to tell Mum! She throws ours away!'

Flipping his bike around, he clambered on. 'I'd better see if we've got any letters. Bye!'

Hilda grinned as she watched him ride away. Fred was a proper case, and no mistake. She'd tell Gordon all about it when he came round.

Indoors, she gathered up her own letters and put them in the rack, and then, smiling to herself, she walked into the kitchen to make a start on dinner.

Now, what could she get Fred for his birthday? Thank goodness she had Gordon to help her think.

'Now then, young Fred,' said Florence Garvey. She eased herself up slowly from the flower beds. There were days when she felt all of her ninety-one years, but she hadn't been brought up to give into such feelings. Things took a little longer nowadays, but one didn't give up.

'Active mind, active body,' she could hear her father saying. He'd lived till he was 103 and he was still walking three miles a day and doing his physical jerks in the morning. He'd been a PT Instructor in the Army, and it had given him a philosophy for life that he'd never forgotten.

'Hello, Miss Garvey,' Fred said, leaning his bike against the garden wall.

'What can I do for you today,' asked Florence. 'Come for a question?'

'No, thank you. I've come to invite you to my party.'

'A party?'

‘Yup,’ said Fred. ‘It’s my birthday next Saturday and I’m having a party.’

‘Well, now, that is exciting.’

‘It’s going to be brilliant. There’ll be balloons an’ that and probably party hats and loads of food and crackers.’

‘I see,’ said Florence. She bent closer to whisper. ‘Do your mum and dad actually know?’

‘Course,’ said Fred. ‘Mum said I can have a party.’

‘Fred?’ In the hallway, John Bunting stood at the bottom of the stairs calling up to his son. ‘Fred? Can you come down for a minute, please?’

Fred’s head appeared over the bannister rail. ‘I’m tidying my bedroom.’

‘That sounds extremely unlikely. Can you come down, please? Mum and I would like a word with you.’

John returned to the kitchen, where his wife, Grace, was sitting at the table.

‘We can’t disappoint him,’ she said. ‘We’ll have to go ahead with it.’

‘He can’t go making arrangements without telling us, Grace,’ John said. ‘Next thing you know, he’ll have volunteered us all for some television show, or something.’

Grace giggled.

‘It’s not funny,’ John said. ‘I shan’t say too much, but he does need to know.’

Grace bit her lip. ‘Of course, dear.’

‘And have you thought about the work? Goodness knows how many he’s invited.’

‘We’ve got lovely neighbours,’ Grace said. ‘I’m sure they’ll all bring something.’

‘I know we have, and I love to see them, but I’d rather know about it first. What if Florence hadn’t phoned us and everyone had just turned up on Saturday?’

Grace started to laugh. ‘Oh, sorry. But they know what he’s like. They would have mentioned it.’

‘Hmm,’ said John. He turned as Fred walked into the kitchen, bouncing a ball. ‘Ball away, please, Fred. I want to talk to you.’

Fred bounced the ball twice more. ‘Ninety-nine … a hundred!’

‘I shan’t ask you again, Fred. Now, what’s all this about a party on Saturday? We’ve had a phone call from Miss Garvey …’

‘Brilliant! I knew she’d come!’

‘Fred, dear,’ Grace began, gently. ‘I didn’t say you could have a party next Saturday.’

Fred gawped. ‘You did, Mum! I said can I have a party and you said, ‘We’ll see.’

‘Precisely,’ said his father. ‘We’ll see. Not yes.’

‘But it’s the same thing,’ Fred protested.

‘No,’ said John, firmly. ‘It isn’t.’

‘It was last week.’

John looked at him. ‘What d’you mean?’

‘You remember, Dad. You were eating those peanuts and Mum said, ‘Don’t they give you indigestion?’ And you said, ‘We’ll see’. And then you got indigestion.’

For a moment or two, John stared at him.

‘He’s got you there,’ Grace said, trying hard not to laugh. She put a hand on Fred’s shoulder. ‘Look, sweetheart. What dad means is you’ve should have asked us before you invited everyone. And we need to know who you’ve invited. Okay?’

‘I’ve got a list,’ he said. He dashed from the kitchen to return seconds later with a scrap of paper.

‘Good heavens,’ said John and Grace together, as they stared at the list. ‘Is everyone coming?’

‘Yup,’ he said. ‘Although Mr Pugh might be at a meeting with Phil Atterly.’

Grace wrapped her arms around him . ‘Oh dear. You’ll be the death of me, you really will. Come on love, we’ve got a lot of party things to sort out.’

The following Saturday brought glorious sunshine and bubbling clouds. Fortunately, a handy wind kept shuffling them along before they could settle over the village.

In Fred’s garden, his birthday party was in full swing. Grown-ups chatted, children shrieked and giggled and everyone rallied round to help Grace and John put on a marvellous birthday tea.

Adelaide Flowers had made a lucky dip tub out of an old linen basket filled with polystyrene shapes and Carmel and Rose Prentice, owners of The Hot Cross Bun, had baked some special treats.

‘Now then, Fred,’ said Florence Garvey, as she sat with Jacob Henry enjoying her tea. ‘Here comes Mum with your cake. Time to blow out your candles.’

Standing before the table, Fred dragged in a long breath and blew so hard on the candles, four of them fell over.

Later that afternoon, when all was cleared and goodbyes had been said, Fred sat with his sister Lucy, looking at his birthday presents.

'They're brilliant, Lu,' he said. 'And you can play with them as well. Except the Lego which you can't play with because it's too old. You can play with the fairy spaceship that Miss Dunbar made me, 'cause it's got flowers on it and I'll play with the spy kit that Mr Pugh gave me. It's got invisible ink and everything. I s'pect I shall belong to a secret club soon like he does.'

'I can play, too,' said Lucy.

'You can play if we're not on a secret mission,' Fred said, airily. 'But other times, you can be my psychic.'

'I think you mean sidekick, Fred,' said his mum, as she walked by.

'And,' said Fred, 'we've got to start practising with the puppets Miss Garvey bought me, so we can put on a show. They're called Marie Antionettes and you have to wiggle them.'

'It's marionettes,' his dad called.

Frowning, Fred stood up and put his hands on his hips. 'Come on, Lu,' he whispered. 'Let's go upstairs, where we can look at my things on our own.'

Lucy held up a strangely-shaped wooden object. 'Shall I bring this?'

‘Yup,’ said Fred. ‘That’s my most special-ist present. Mr Meredith made it, so it could be anything, but be careful, ‘cause Mr Meredith’s things break a lot.’

‘Why?’

Fred shook his head, sagely. ‘No one knows.’

Fred On the Case

As Eleanor Everett walked up the hallway that morning in answer to the doorbell, she wondered if it might be the postman. She was waiting on a couple of parcels, plants she'd ordered from a seed catalogue. As she approached the door, she glanced through the glass panel at the top, and frowned. There didn't seem to be any one there.

The doorbell rang again.

'Just coming!'

She opened the door. On the doorstep stood a small boy. He was dressed in jeans and a tee-shirt, his hair neatly combed into place, save for one tuft, which stuck out at an odd angle. Looking up at her with sparkling eyes, Fred Bunting was unusually spick and span, but it was, she reminded herself, still only ten thirty.

Eleanor had thought often over the years about a move to the country and retirement had seemed the right time. The last property on her list of viewings, Cowslip Cottage and its beautiful garden, was everything she'd dreamed of. Somehow, it just seemed right.

The village had welcomed her. Several of the residents had already called by, two of whom had been Fred Bunting and his mother.

'Hello, Miss.'

She smiled down at him. 'Hello there, Fred. How are you?'

'I'm fine, thank you.'

'And your mum? How is she?'

'She's fine, thank you.'

'That's good.'

Fred continued to stand on the doorstep, and she wondered if he had his sights set on another slice of the coconut cake he'd devoured on his previous visit. The cake had been a gift from Carmel and Rose Prentice, the local bakers, whose cakes, he'd informed her, were brilliant.

'Was there something you wanted, Fred?'

Fred shifted from one foot to the other. 'Mum asked me to give you this recipe for gingerbread,' he said. 'The one you were talking about.' He produced a neatly written sheet of paper.

Eleanor leaned out to glance down the road, where, in the distance, she could just make out the figure of Fred's mum giving her a wave. She waved back.

'Tell your Mum I said thank you very much,' said Eleanor. 'Would you like a piece of cake, Fred?'

To her surprise, he said, 'No, thank you very much.'

'You have lovely manners, Fred.'

'I know, it's just natural. Miss, is your name Esmerelda?'

'No,' she said.

Fred looked thoughtful. 'Oh.'

'It's Eleanor.'

'Oh.'

She was about to ask if it was important, when he gave a sigh and said, 'I've got to go now, we're having lunch early today 'cause Mum's taking Gran to the Clinic to have her onion done. Bye!'

Grabbing his bicycle, he hopped on board and began to pedal.

'Bye Fred.'

Eleanor watched him cycle away, then with a smile, she slowly closed the door.

She'd just reached the kitchen, when the doorbell rang again. Surely not. It couldn't be.

Her heart lifted as she spotted a familiar red uniform through the door. The postman.

'Morning! Parcel for you?'

'Good morning. Thank you very much.'

The postman turned and almost fell over Fred, who was right behind him. 'Oh, sorry there, son.'

'Miss,' said Fred, as the postman closed the gate. 'Did your hair used to be ginger? You know, before it was grey?'

'No, I'm afraid it wasn't. It was brown.'

Fred looked slightly crestfallen. 'Oh. Ok, then. Bye!'

Watching him cycle away a second time, Eleanor struggled to think of any possible reason for his question, but after a few moments admitted defeat.

Putting the parcel down in the hall, she slipped on her coat. Now she could pop to the shop and pick up some milk.

Sometime later, she was walking slowly back along the road. As usual, the pint of milk had turned into a few things more, and the basket was heavy.

'Oh, no…'

The voice came from just beside her. Eleanor stopped, grateful for a chance to put down the basket, and looked around.

'Not again,' said the voice.

Stepping forward, Eleanor peered over the hedge. A man was there, crouching low to the ground, staring intently at a bush.

'Excuse me,' she ventured, 'but are you all right?'

A head of thick silver hair turned slightly to look, then pushing down on his knees, the man stiffly straightened up.

'Sorry,' she said. 'I didn't mean to disturb you.'

'That's quite all right,' he said. 'I was muttering. Something appears to be attacking this bush. It's covered in buds, but before they get a chance to open, something's eating them.'

'Oh dear. Some sort of insect, d'you think?'

He shrugged. 'Heaven only knows,' he said. 'It's a mystery. Every day I come out and there's one or two missing.' He turned suddenly and held out his hand. 'Forgive me, you must be our new neighbour at Cowslip Cottage. Miss Everett, is it? I'm Henry. Henry Matthews.'

They shook hands. 'Pleased to meet you, Henry. Do call me Eleanor. I see news travels fast in the village.'

Henry laughed. 'It certainly does. Mind you, we have got our own town crier. Young fellow name of Fred. I expect you've met him?'

'I have,' she said. 'A young gentleman who's rather fond of cake.'

'That'll be him. A lovely lad, and bright as a button.'

A bell interrupted their conversation. 'Hello,' said Henry, 'it's the man himself.'

Fred's bike screeched to a halt beside them. 'Hello, Mr Matthews. Hello, Miss.'

Henry beamed at him. 'Hello young Fred,' he said. 'What have you got there?'

'A pipe,' he said. 'It's Mum's bubble pipe. She says you can't buy them these days, so I can use it if I want, so I thought I'd bring it in case there's a mystery to solve. Sherlock Holmes always has a pipe.'

'Well now, that's a bit of luck, because there's a mystery here right enough,' said Henry. He pointed at the empty space where a bud had once been. 'Something, or someone, is stealing the buds.'

Dismounting from his bike, Fred pulled a magnifying glass from his pocket and stepped across to examine the bush.

'D'you often solve mysteries, Fred?' Eleanor asked.

'Sometimes,' he said. 'Sometimes I help Mr Matthews. He was a Spector, you know.'

She assumed Fred meant Inspector. Henry looked a little substantial for the spirit world.

'He's Santa, as well.'

Eleanor looked at Henry with raised eyebrows. 'Really? Now, that's what I call an active retirement.'

Henry grinned. 'I helped out at the Children's Party last year when Jacob went down with flu.'

'Are you going to wear that, Mr Matthews?'

Henry looked down at Fred. 'Wear what?'

'Your Santa outfit. You could wear it to the Fancy Dress.'

'I'm not going to the Fancy Dress.'

Fred looked devastated. 'But you got to. You got to go to the Fancy Dress. Everyone's going.'

Henry shook his head. 'It's not really my cup of tea, Fred.'

'But they'll have other stuff. Squash n'that. Mum said. You could go as Sherlock Holmes. You can borrow my pipe if you want.'

He held out the pipe.

'That's really kind of you, Fred, but I think I'll give it a miss this time.'

'But if you don't *go*,' Fred protested in a loud whisper, 'then who's going to take Miss?'

His eyes flicked toward Eleanor. For a moment or two longer, he looked at them both, then leaped on his bicycle and rode away, leaving Henry and Eleanor with an awkward silence.

'Please,' Eleanor began, 'don't feel you have to.'

'Well, of course, I'd be delighted …'

'But if you weren't going to go … it isn't really my kind of thing either, to be honest.'

The silence returned, then mercifully, they both started to smile.

'He means well,' said Henry, watching Fred in the distance.

'I know. I think he just wants us to go.'

'Bless him. I suppose we should be flattered.' Henry looked at Eleanor. 'You know, if you would like to go, I'd be delighted to accompany you, though maybe I should mention I'm not the best dancer in the world.'

Eleanor hesitated. Dancing really wasn't her thing, either. It was years since she'd danced, she'd be bound to tread on his feet.

'I'm not much of a dancer, either,' she confessed. 'It's been years.'

His eyes twinkled. 'I'll give it a go if you will.'

She smiled. 'Why not? Thank you, Henry, I'd be delighted.'

'Lovely. I'll pick you up about …'

'I've got it, Mr Matthews!' Fred had returned like a whirlwind, his face shining. 'I've got it!'

'I have it,' Eleanor corrected.

Fred glanced at her. 'Well, I bet your idea's not as good as mine.'

Henry bit his lip. 'What exactly do you have, Fred?'

'An idea,' he said. 'What you can go as.'

'I see.'

'You can go as Superman and Esmerelda,' he announced, proudly. 'Course, Miss' name isn't really

Esmerelda. It'd be wicked if it was, but it don't matter, we can pretend.'

He turned to Eleanor. 'Esmerelda is the lady in Lunchpack of Notre Dame, Miss, and she's usually with Cassie Modo, but I thought Mr Matthews might not know bell-ringing, so he could go as Superman, 'cause he flies 'n' all. Mum said you could go as Fred Astaire and Roy Rogers, but Miss's hair wasn't ginger.'

There was a moment's silence, while Eleanor fought against a smile, then she took a deep breath and said, 'Well, that's very kind of you, and we'll bear it in mind, but I expect we can find some costumes.'

Disappointment clouded Fred's face. 'Oh.'

'I'm amazed,' Henry said, quickly, 'that a busy fellow like yourself has time to bother with things like that. What about the case?'

He waved a hand toward the bush. Fred's face lit up. 'I'm on it, Sir!'

'Very good, Constable Fred,' said Henry. 'I shall expect a report in due course. In the meantime, perhaps you would care for a cup of tea, Eleanor?'

Standing in the hallway on a sunny Saturday morning, Ex-Chief Inspector Henry Matthews ran a brush over his costume. Admiral of the Fleet.

He hoped he wouldn't let Eleanor down. They'd become such good friends, and he felt sure she was going to look wonderful as Queen Victoria.

The ring at the bell made him jump.

Fred stood on the doorstep, holding a scrap of paper. 'I've solved it!' he said, triumphantly. 'I set up a yobbo and caught him in the act. Here's my report.'

Henry took the scrap of paper and read it. On it was scrawled one word. 'Squirel.'

Fred suddenly tugged at his arm. Before their eyes, the culprit had appeared. The squirrel ran down, plucked off a bud and proceeded to eat it.

'See!'

'Well done, Constable Fred,' said Henry. He pulled a pound coin from his pocket and gave it to him.

'Wow! Thank you very much, Mr Matthews! Are you and Miss going tonight?'

'We are indeed. We'll see you there.'

Outside on the path, Fred leaned his bike over to allow a ginger cat to leap into the basket.

'I told you, Nappy,' he said, as they cycled home. 'Mr Matthews and Miss are going to get married now and it's all thanks to me.'

He turned the coin over in his hand. 'C'mon,' he said. 'We can buy that eye patch. I'm going as a pirate, and Grandad's promised to make me a cutlet.' He glanced down at the cat. 'You can be my parrot, if you want.'

Fred and the Pumpkin

'Wow, Miss Dunbar, that's the biggest pumpkin I've ever seen.'

Hilda Dunbar looked up from her digging.

Fred Bunting was crouching down beside the pumpkin patch, staring at the prize pumpkin Hilda had so lovingly nurtured. It was her best effort yet and she already had it earmarked for the Autumn Show.

'Don't touch it, Fred, there's a good boy. It's a bit fragile.'

'I won't touch it, Miss Dunbar. It's huge, though, isn't it?'

Hilda nodded, watching nervously as he leaned a little closer. Remembering a bag of toffees in her pocket, she quickly offered him one.

'Certainly is,' she said. 'Let you into a little secret, Fred, I'm entering it for the Autumn Show this year.'

'Wow!'

Hilda liked Fred Bunting, everyone did. He had a bright, enquiring mind and wanted to know everything. Sometimes his imagination ran away with him a little, but in Hilda's opinion, a good imagination opened up whole new worlds for a child. If they believed in fairies and Santa Claus, then why not? Real life arrived quite soon enough.

She waved at Fred's dad, working hard on his allotment next door.

'D'you know, Fred,' Hilda said, confidentially, 'I'm actually beginning to wonder if this pumpkin might change into a coach one evening. You know, like in Cinderella.'

Fred stopped chewing, and stared. Leaning closer, he whispered, 'Cinderella's only pretend, Miss Dunbar, but it doesn't matter, I won't tell that you didn't know. I've got to help Dad with the potatoes now. Bye!'

Despite feeling slightly breathless, as one so often did after Fred's departure, Hilda couldn't help smiling.

So much for my prized theories, she thought.

'I know what we can call him, Miss Dunbar!'
It was the following morning and Fred was careering down Hilda's garden path.

Just around the corner from Fred's house, Hilda Dunbar's cottage was the first on the edge of the green. It was small and neat. A path of crazy paving wound its way through a carefully tended rose garden and two borders, bursting with late autumn blooms. Four gnomes kept watch and unbeknown to anyone but Hilda, three tiny fairy cottages nestled in the flowerbeds.

With a neat snip, Hilda clipped a dead head from a rose bush.

'Call who, Fred?'

'The pumpkin,' he said, screeching to a halt beside her. 'I know what we can call him!'

'Oh, I see,' said Hilda, trying not to smile. Perhaps she had been right after all. The same child who didn't accept the idea of a pumpkin coach, was now giving the pumpkin a name. How delightful.

'Well, I hadn't thought of giving it a name,' she said. 'But it's a good idea. What did you have in mind?'

Fred pulled an apple from his pocket and bit it. 'Eisenstein.'

Hilda paused. Of all the names she'd expected him to say, Eisenstein came rather low on the list. She'd expected something liked Peter or Percival, maybe even Superman, but Eisenstein?

'Any particular reason?'

Fred chewed rhythmically. 'Cause he was a genius,' he said, as though that should be more than reason enough.

Hilda nodded. 'Well, yes, I suppose he was,' she said. 'In his own field.'

He swallowed. 'Did he live in a field, then?'

'Oh no, it means he was very good at the particular thing he did.'

'He was brilliant!' said Fred, with enthusiasm. 'He knew all about people's relatives. He had a famous theory about it. I think he might have started one of those sites where you find your family tree. Grandad's doing our family tree right now and he says we might be related to Alfred the Great. He was a king in the olden days who burnt cakes 'n' that.'

'Well, that is one of the stories about Alfred the Great,' Hilda conceded, 'but of course he was a very clever man, too, and a good King.'

'Was he?'

'He was. I saw a programme about him. I'll refresh my memory and tell you about him one day. Now, about Eisenstein …'

'The pumpkin?'

'Yes, the pumpkin. I'm sure the name you're thinking of is Einstein. He was a physicist, who developed the theory of relativity.'

Fred gazed at her. 'Wow!' he said. 'You know *loads*. What's a fizzy cyst?'

Hilda's desire to impart knowledge wavered a little. She knew who Einstein was and roughly what he did, but that was all. Even more worrying, Fred might ask her to explain the theory of relativity, and whilst there were probably a great many people for whom that would be a walk in the park, Hilda wasn't one of them.

'Ask your Grandad,' she said. 'He'll tell you. So, we'll call the pumpkin Einstein then, shall we?'

'Ok.' Jumping on his bike, Fred cycled up the path. At the gate, he stopped. 'So, who's Eisenstein, then?'

Hilda took a deep breath. 'He was a famous film director.'

'Oh,' said Fred. 'Thank you.'

'You're welcome. Bye-bye.'

Fred cycled out of the gate, then stopped again. 'Did Eisenstein do Star Wars, Miss Dunbar?'

Hilda coughed. 'No, Fred. No, he didn't do Star Wars …'

She teetered for a moment on the brink. Should she mention Battleship Potemkin and Ivan the Terrible? On balance, she thought not.

'He did other films,' she said. 'Historical ones. A long while ago now.'

'Oh. Ok. Bye!'

It was almost a week before Fred paid another visit.

Hilda had been at her allotment early that morning, and after giving Einstein his regular dose of her secret plant food, she was now having a general tidy-up. At eleven-thirty, Gordon Pugh popped across from his own vegetable plot and asked if Hilda would, perhaps, care to share some tea, and the muffins he'd made the day before?

Hilda was delighted. Strictly between Hilda and the fairies, she rather liked Gordon. He was a gentleman, and a nature lover like herself, kind, thoughtful, and most interesting to talk to. He kept an open mind about things and would never dismiss things out of hand, purely because of popular opinion.

Hilda and Gordon had been enjoying tea and blueberry muffins in each other's company for almost an hour, when Fred and his father arrived at the allotments.

Fred wasted no time in popping across to see Einstein, though Hilda strongly suspected the blueberry muffins were the stronger attraction. When it came to muffins, he had a better nose than a bloodhound.

'I love blueberry muffins!'

Gordon offered the tin. 'Would you like one, Fred? Plenty to go around.'

'Yes please, Mr Pugh. Thank you very much!'

Hilda felt relieved, not only because of Fred's beautiful manners, but because he'd remembered the correct pronunciation of Gordon's surname. At the Annual Show the year before, Fred had told everyone that Mr Pug had won first prize in the leek category.

'He's growing, Miss Dunbar!'

Hilda turned to see Fred leaning perilously close to Einstein the ever-expanding pumpkin.

'He is,' she agreed, a little nervously.

Gordon looked over. 'Another muffin?'

Fred peered even closer at Einstein. 'No thank you, Mr Pugh,' he said. 'Mum says I mustn't have too many snacks today, because we're having dinner early at Nan and Grandad's. Grandad's going to tell me all about the family tree, and I'm going to ask him about the theory of relatives.'

Gordon gave Hilda a quick glance.

'We were discussing it the other day,' Hilda explained. 'When Fred was thinking of a name for the pumpkin. Fred, do come away, there's a good boy, in case you slip.'

Fred squinted at the glossy orange skin. 'There's a bug on 'im.'

Hilda sprang to her feet. 'What? Where?'

'Oh no, it's all right,' said Fred, carelessly. 'It's a blueberry out of my muffin.'

He picked it off and popped it into his mouth.

Hilda sat down again with a bump and closed her eyes.

'Thank goodness the show's next week,' said Gordon, smiling.

'He means well,' she whispered. 'But I just know there's going to be an accident, and he'll fall in head-first.'

Gordon chuckled.

'It's ok,' said Fred, wandering over. 'I've given 'im the once over, Miss Dunbar and there's nothing on 'im. Course, there's another week yet, so I'll come over as often as I can, and I'll bring my bug-catcher with me, just in case.'

'A bug-catcher, Fred? What's that, then?'

Fred looked at Gordon. 'It's what you catch bugs with,' he said.

The day of the Autumn show started misty.

'Seasons of mist and mellow fruitfulness,' Hilda said to herself, as she packed Einstein pumpkin into the back of her car. 'Maybe this will be my year.'

It had been a rather busy week. All the allotment holders had selected their prize specimens for the show. Hilda had entered two of her homemade jams in the preserves section and some apples and figs, but her best hope, she felt, was Einstein.

Fred's dad had also been busy with last minute preparations and had been over the allotment most days, so Fred had been on constant bug alert, but somehow, despite it all, Einstein had survived.

By eleven, the warm sunshine had burnt off the autumn mist and large crowds had gathered for the event.

By two-thirty, the judging was complete, and everyone sat waiting until they could enter the marquee to view the results.

'Not long now,' said Gordon, as he and Hilda sat by the refreshment tent. 'Not very confident about the leeks this year, but you never know.'

'I'm sure they'll do very well.' Hilda glanced across to see the Bunting family waiting for the results. 'There were such wonderful pumpkins there this year, I don't think Einstein stands a chance. Fred will be dreadfully disappointed.'

'Hello,' said Gordon. 'Here comes the man of the hour.'

Fred was approaching, clutching a small plastic scoop. 'Here it is, Mr Pugh,' said Fred, 'I brought my bug-catcher, just in case someone needs it. I got loads, look!'

He held it up, a little too near their cups for Hilda's liking. The plastic scoop was alive with insects of all kinds.

'You can look, but it'll have to be quick, 'cause I've got to let them go. Found one just like *that*,' he said, pointing to a beetle, 'on Einstein.'

Hilda's heart sank. 'You didn't.'

Fred leaned into whisper. 'S'all right,' he said. 'I moved it before they did the judges.'

'You're a dear.'

Fred shrugged. 'I know,' he said. 'It's just natural.'

A sudden thought flooded Hilda's mind. 'Fred … the beetle you found on Einstein. Where did you put it?'

'On that other big pumpkin, next to 'im,' he said.

Ten minutes later, as they filed into the marquee, Hilda's heart was beating wildly. What if that beetle had done its damage?

She looked down at her rosette. Second place! More than she could have hoped for! Guiltily, she glanced at the larger pumpkin beside it. A shiny gold rosette announced first place.

Hilda breathed a sigh of relief. There was no sign of the beetle.

'Congratulations, Hilda.'

Hilda turned to see Gordon. 'Well?' she asked.

'Two firsts and a second.'

'Oh, that's wonderful,' she said. 'Well done, Gordon.'

'Thank you. Actually, Hilda, I was thinking, as we both have something to celebrate …'

'We did brilliant, Miss Dunbar!' Fred's head appeared like a jack-in-the-box. 'We got second!'

Hilda patted his shoulder. 'We certainly did. And all thanks to you, Fred.'

'I only did bug watch,' said Fred, generously. 'Anyway, Grandad says we might be related to the Duke of Burgundy as well, now. Bye!'

Before Hilda could reply, Fred had vanished, back to his family.

'That's on at the moment,' said Gordon. 'At the old Regal in the town.'

‘What is?’

‘Passport to Pimlico. About the Duke of Burgundy.’

‘Oh my goodness, I haven’t seen that in years.’

‘Nor me,’ he said. ‘I wondered if you’d care to go this evening? Have a spot of dinner maybe?’

Hilda’s heart sang. ‘I’d be delighted,’ she said.

Fred's Firework Night

'We're having a Catherine Wheel,' said a voice.

On the other side of the garden fence, Gerald Douglas paused for a moment, then forked more leaves into the wheelbarrow.

'And a Roman Candle,' said the voice.

Gerald sighed. Fred was talking at him, and whilst he wholeheartedly approved of a child's thirst for knowledge, sometimes, just sometimes, he wished Fred had a Pause Button.

'*And,*' said Fred. 'We've got Golden Rain.'

Gerald turned. Fred was hanging over the fence. 'Rain?'

'Yup. And it's going to be golden.'

'Oh, I see,' he said. 'You mean the fireworks.'

'Yup.'

Gerald nodded. 'Well, when I was a boy …'

'Was that ages and ages ago?'

'A few years,' he said.

'How many years?'

'A few.'

Experience had taught him that where Fred was concerned, keeping things vague was the way to go.

He ploughed on. 'As I was saying, when I was a boy, we had fireworks called Bengal Matches and Jumping Jacks.'

'Did they jump?'

'Yes, they did. All over the place. Once you lit it, it shot about, banging and sparking. Sometimes, they leaped into the air and landed on people, which is probably why you don't see them anymore. They were a bit dangerous.'

Fred frowned. 'Why were they called Jacks?'

'I don't really know.'

'D'you think a man called Jack invented them?'

Gerald could feel himself losing a grip on the conversation. Time to resort to one-word answers.

'Possibly.'

'It's ok if you don't know,' said Fred. 'I'll ask Grandad. He knows everything.'

'That's fine, then,' said Gerald. He took a deep breath and picked up his fork. 'Best get on.'

'What's Bengal Matches?'

Gerald put his fork down again. 'They were a long match that burned different colours,' he said. 'Red and … green, if memory serves. You held them, like a sparkler.'

'What else did they do?'

'Nothing else,' he said. 'They just burned.'

'Oh.'

Fred looked so disappointed, Gerald found himself volunteering something else.

'We had squibs, too,' he said.

Fred's eyes opened wide. 'Wow! We're having chipolatas.'

'You don't eat a squib, it's a small firework. It used to hiss for ages before it went bang. It's where we get the phrase 'damp squib' from.'

'Squids are always damp, Mr Douglas. They live in the sea.'

Warming to his subject, Gerald took a step closer to the fence. 'Not squid, Fred, *squib*. A damp squib is a term they apply to something that's disappointing. If squibs got damp – which they often did in November – they wouldn't go off, d'you see? So they were a disappointment.'

'Wow, Mr Douglas, you know loads.'

Gerald gave a modest cough. 'Well … it's just something I remember.'

'What else d'you remember?'

'I remember tiny bars of chocolate that cost a ha'penny.'

'What's a ha'penny?'

Gerald realised he'd walked right into what could become another long conversation.

'Ask your Grandad,' he said. 'He'll tell you.' He picked up his fork once more. 'Anyway, nice having a chat Fred, but I must get on. I expect your tea's ready.'

He returned to his wheelbarrow. When he glanced back, Fred had disappeared behind the fence.

Shortly after, it started to rain and Gerald watched solemnly through the window as his neatly sculptured pile of leaves turned to a soggy mess.

The telephone rang, and he walked across to pick it up. It was Jim from the Darts team.

'Gerry?'

'Hello Jim,' he said. 'How's things?'

'Stefan's broken his arm,' Jim said, abruptly.

'You're kidding.'

'Fraid not. We are now one short for the match.'

Gerald closed his eyes. It was the final on Saturday. They'd fought their way through the heats and now, they were just a whisper away from the trophy. He visualised the trophy, gleaming and shining, behind the bar of The Three Crowns, until the image crumbled. Stefan was one of their best players. They were done for.

'What about Pearl? She's a cracking player.'

'On holiday.'

'Bill?'

'Laid up with flu.'

'Oh, poor Bill. Ok, leave it with me, Jim,' he said. 'I'll give it some thought.'

'Hello, Mr Douglas!'

It was the following morning. The rainclouds had cleared away, and now it was crisp and sunny. Ideal weather for Firework Night.

Gerald was off to the shops for a paper and a couple of delicious rolls from the bakers. He might treat himself to a London Cheesecake as well, he thought. Good brain food, cheesecakes were, and he needed it if he was to solve the problem of the darts match.

Turning at the gate, he blinked as the sun reflected off Fred's handlebars, straight into his eyes.

'Hello, Fred.'

'We've bought some more fireworks for tonight,' said Fred, balancing his bike against the gatepost. 'And we've got some food. What are you bringing?'

Gerald shook his head. 'I'm not going to the Bonfire.'

'Why?'

'I'm getting a little old for fireworks. They're for children, really.'

'They're not for children,' Fred said. 'Mum and Dad are going, and Nan and Grandad. We're all going. And we're taking loads of food. Mum and Nan are taking extra for the elderly people at Chestnut Lodge.'

'Well, that's very kind of them.'

'So you won't be the only old person there,' Fred said. 'My Nan and Grandad are old, too. You can come with us.'

'Well, thank you for the invite, Fred -'

'Brilliant! I'll tell Mum!'

Before Gerald could say any more, Fred leaped on his bike, cycled quickly down his path and in through the back gate.

Gerald put a hand to his forehead. Another problem. What was he going to do?

Gerald spent most of the morning debating whether to pop next door and politely decline Fred's offer, but somehow, he never quite made it. Somewhere at the back of his mind, he felt it might be rude to refuse.

John and Grace Bunting were lovely neighbours, always offering to help. What if Fred had told them, and Grace had already made extra food for him?

By one o'clock, Gerald decided he would have to go to the village Bonfire party, but he couldn't go empty-handed. Everyone else would bring something.

At two o'clock, he was walking back down to the shops. At three o'clock, he stepped back through his front door with a carrier bag. Fireworks, a large box. Sparklers, three packs, including those amazing new coloured ones he'd never seen before. He put the box on the table. Perhaps he should just check the contents to see if they were ok.

By four o'clock, Gerald realised he'd been so enthralled by the fireworks, he'd forgotten to have any lunch. He was devouring a hasty sandwich, when he heard Fred's voice in the garden. 'Mr Douglas!'

Gerald swallowed quickly and stepped outside.

'Mum says to say we're going at six o'clock,' said Fred. 'She said don't bother bringing any food 'cause we've got plenty, soup and rolls, jacket potatoes with cheese, though you can leave the cheese off if you want, and beans and burgers and pizzas and chipolatas. Nan's doing tea and scones and things and we'll meet you by the front gate.'

'Thank you!' called Gerald.

Fred's head disappeared, but not before he'd yelled, 'And don't move the leaves, Mr Douglas!'

When Gerald walked out of his front door at five minutes to six, the Bunting family were packing enough food to feed an army, into the car.

'Hello Mr Douglas!' Fred cried. 'Dad! It's Mr Douglas!'

His father looked up. 'Thank you, Fred,' he said. 'I can see it's Mr Douglas. Now, you go and help Mum.'

He turned to Gerald. 'Hello, Gerry,' he said. 'I do hope Fred didn't cajole you into coming this evening. He means well.'

'Not at all, John.' Gerald held up the carrier bag. 'I … um … brought some fireworks.'

'Wonderful. The more the merrier.'

Gerald had often seen the glow of the village bonfire light up the sky and heard the distant echoes, but now, standing before the blaze, the warmth of the flames and the smell of the fireworks transported him straight back to his childhood. He was a boy again, drawing patterns in the air with a sparkler.

'Would you like a toffee apple, Mr Douglas?'

Gerald looked down at Fred, clutching a small apple on a stick. 'Nan makes them. They're brilliant.'

'Well, that's very kind,' he said. 'Tell your Nan thank you. I haven't had one of these since I was a child.'

A huge rocket whistled into the air and exploded in a crescendo of stars.

'Fireworks came from China, first off,' said Fred. 'My grandad told me. He knows everything.'

'I wish,' murmured a voice. Frank Bunting had appeared behind them. 'Now then, Fred,' he said. 'Are you enjoying the fireworks?'

'They're brilliant, Grandad!'

'They certainly are. Now, off you go, your mum wants you. She said something about hot dogs?'

'Yay!' Fred raced across to his mum at the table.

Frank Bunting turned to Gerald. 'Sorry about that, Gerry,' he said. 'He means well.'

Gerald grinned. 'No apology necessary. He's a lovely lad and he obviously adores you, which is just as it should be.'

'I adore him, too,' said Frank. 'And I know I should be flattered, but sometimes it's not easy, living up to his expectations. He's got me down as a sort of cross between Einstein and Houdini.'

'Tell him your Superman costume's in the wash.'

'I daren't do that,' Frank said. 'He'll expect me to fly.'

They both laughed.

Another rocket lit up the sky.

'How's the darts going? John says you're in the team for The Three Crowns this year.'

Gerald nodded. 'Yes. We're in the final on Saturday, but it's a bit in doubt, now. One of our best players broke his arm.'

'Oh dear, that's bad luck. Look, if you're stuck, I used to play a bit.'

'Really?'

'Yes. I'm not exactly championship standard, but I'll give it a shot.'

'That would be wonderful, Frank, thank you so much.'

'My pleasure.'

The faint smell of smoke was still lingering in the air, as Gerald stepped out into his garden the following morning. The sun was sparkling on the frosted grass and delicate cobwebs hung like diamond necklaces on the bushes.

He'd phoned Jim first thing to tell him the news, and Jim had been delighted at the mention of Frank's name. Frank Bunting, it seemed, had been well-known on the local darts circuit.

Sipping his coffee, Gerald felt at peace with the world.

'Hello, Mr Douglas!'

Gerald looked up. Fred's face was peering over the fence.

'Good morning, Fred,' he said. 'Did you enjoy the fireworks?'

'They were brilliant!' Leaning further over the fence, Fred looked up and down the garden. 'What have you done with Herbie, Mr Douglas?'

'Who's Herbie?'

'The hedgehog who was living in your leaves.'

Gerald almost dropped his cup. 'Oh, my goodness, Fred, why didn't you tell me?'

'I did,' said Fred. 'I said, 'Don't move the leaves, Mr Douglas', 'cause I'd just seen him going in there, but he wasn't in there before, and it's all *right*, because he came into our garden yesterday. I made a hole for him under the fence and I put him in a little house and he snuggled down. This morning, he ate some dog food, but then he wanted a walk in your garden again. There he is!'

Gerald sighed with relief as he watched what looked like a spikey slipper squeezing back under the fence into Fred's garden.

'I'm going to put him away now,' said Fred, 'cause Grandad said he should be hivernating for the winter. Bye, Mr Douglas!'

Clutching a lukewarm coffee cup, Gerald said two prayers of thanks. One for Herbie, and one for giving him the nerves of steel he needed to live next door to Fred Bunting.

Fred's Christmas Star

Adelaide Flowers watched the flow of silver ink fade into a colourless line.

'No … please last a bit longer. I've only got two cards left to do.'

She shook the pen in a desperate attempt to get it going again. It hiccupped a blot of ink, then faded in and out.

'Blow!'

She pressed it a little too firmly on a spare scrap of paper, but that only made matters worse. She now had a gleaming new silver pen with a bent tip.

'Why, oh why, did I leave Clarissa's card until last?' she cried.

Adelaide looked down at the card she'd chosen especially for Clarissa Crochet. Clarissa always sent such beautiful handmade cards at Christmas. Rumour had it, she started them at Eastertime, and this year, just for once, Adelaide wanted to reciprocate with a card to be remembered.

After a few stressful days trying to make her own, she was forced to admit what she already knew. When it came to card-making, she was not blessed.

Picking up the card she'd bought at the department store in town, she looked at it. It was a sparkling snowy village scene, with tiny lights.

Slowly, she opened it, and read her writing.

'Happy Christmas Clarissa, and a very Hap … New (blot) …ear.'

Adelaide let out a long sigh. Back to the shops for another silver pen, but how on earth was she going to disguise the blot?

Last year, Clarissa's exquisite card had contained a homecooked gingerbread star.

She stared at the blot. A red chocolate bean would cover it nicely.

'Don't be daft,' she told herself. 'No one with common sense would use one of those in a Christmas card. Especially when they're so useful if you run out of lipstick.'

Giggling, she put the card down on the table, picked up her bag and set off down the hall.
She was slipping on her boots, when the doorbell rang.

Adelaide straightened up, and at once recognised the shadow at the door.

Fred Bunting.

Fred was a delightful child, well-mannered, enthusiastic, and perhaps just a little too bright. Could a child be too bright? It was a question that Adelaide, as his teacher, had often asked herself. The answer of course, was no. Enquiring minds should be encouraged. Questions should be answered, even if they were the first of oh, so many.

Taking a breath, she put down her bag and opened the door.

'Hello, Miss,' said Fred.

'Hello there, Fred. How are you?'

'I'm fine.'

'Good. Good.'

He continued to stand on the doorstep.

Adelaide glanced at her watch. The shops would soon be closing. 'Was there something you wanted? Only I need to get to the shops before they close.'

'You can borrow my bike if you want,' he said.

'Well, that's kind of you, Fred, but it's a little icy for bicycles.'

'It's all right,' he said. 'Grandad fitted snow chains for me.'

'Snow chains? On a bicycle?'

'Yup. It's one of his inventions. He can invent anything.'

'Well that's wonderful. Perhaps he can make Santa some for his sleigh one day.'

Fred leaned in to whisper. 'Did you know Santa's not real, Miss?'

Oh, thought Adelaide, what a shame. She always felt a tinge of sadness when a child lost that magic. She started to say, 'Well, yes, Fred, but the little ones …'

Fred shook his head beneath a large woollen hat. 'No,' he said. 'He's definitely not real. I saw him at the shopping centre and it was Mr Wilberforce. I knew it was him because of his ears and I told Mum and she said Mr Wilberforce is helping Santa out this year.'

Adelaide held in a sigh of relief. How close she'd come to letting the cat out of the bag.

'I see,' she said. 'Well, if you'll excuse me, Fred, I must get to the shops.'

'But you haven't got this.' He held out an envelope. 'It's about the Wii.'

Adelaide smiled as she took it. She and Fred's mum, Grace, were fellow members of the village WI. 'You mean the WI.'

'No, the Wii. It's a gaming console. It's what I've asked Santa for in this letter. I forgot to post it at the shops and Mum saw you were just going out, so could you please put it in the box for me?'

'Of course, I will,' she said. 'I'd be happy too. Don't want you to miss out on your Christmas present from Santa, do we?'

Fred stared at her for a moment, then taking a few steps back, he looked down the road to his own house, several doors away. Walking back, he leaned in for another whisper, 'It's all right, Lucy's up there with Mum. It's really Mum and Dad who get the presents, Miss. Santa isn't real, but Lucy thinks he is, so don't say anything. Thank you very much.'

Adelaide frowned. 'But … if you're Mum and Dad get the presents, Fred, why are you writing to Santa?'

'Cause I don't want Lucy to know,' he said. 'When Lucy did her letter, I didn't do one and she cried, so I had to do one, and then when we posted her letter, she wanted me to post mine, but I left it at home, 'cause I wasn't going to post it and she got all upset, so I wondered if you could post it for me if it's no trouble, 'cause she's watching.'

Leaning out from the doorway, Adelaide saw Fred's sister waving. She waved back, letter in her hand.

'Of course, Fred,' she said.

'And, of course,' he called, as he walked up the path. 'If there is a Santa after all, I might get two lots of presents.'

Somehow, Adelaide held in the laugh until she'd shut the door. She felt slightly exhausted. Where Fred was concerned, it was a feeling she knew only too well.

The following morning, Adelaide looked out of her window to see children's prayers up and down the country being answered. It was snowing.

'How delightful,' she said. 'A white Christmas.'

She picked up the bunch of Christmas cards and popped them into her bag. Thankfully, the blot on Clarissa's card was no longer a problem. The village shop had an almost identical card, with lights!

The first card wouldn't be wasted, of course, Adelaide hadn't been brought up to waste things. Popped in a frame, it would make a nice Christmas picture.

Feeling at peace with the world, she set off for the shops, thrilling at the tickle of snowflakes on her face.

'Morning, Adelaide!'

Adelaide looked through the flakes to see Nick Best, Headteacher at the school. She smiled. She and Nick had worked together for many years and were very close friends. In Adelaide's opinion, he was an excellent Headteacher, a warm, friendly man with a wonderful sense of humour.

'Morning Nick,' she said. 'Enjoying the snow?'

'I am,' he said. 'Just what the doctor ordered for Christmas. Except for poor old Henry, of course.'

'Henry Wilberforce?'

Nick nodded. 'Slipped over on the ice yesterday. Broke his ankle.'

'Oh no,' she said. 'Poor Henry. I must nip along and see how he is … oh! Who's doing Santa, then?'

'Give you three guesses.'

Adelaide chuckled. 'I see. Well, I always said that name would catch up with you one day. And that beard.'

He laughed and ran a hand along his snowy beard, a beard he kept closely cropped because, he had once confided to Adelaide, it invited too many questions from the children at Christmastime.

'Will you be Santa at the Christmas party as well?'

He nodded. 'For my pains,' he said. 'Best be on my way, I'm starting in ten minutes.'

'Good luck,' she called.

As she walked home through the thickening snow, Adelaide couldn't help wondering how long it would take Fred to recognise the new Santa. Best cover your ears, Nick, she thought.

The subject of her thoughts loomed through the snowflakes as she was walking back down her drive.

'Hello, Miss!'

'Ah, Fred. I was just thinking about you.'

'Why?'

Adelaide's mind raced. 'Snow,' she said. 'I was just thinking how lovely the snow is for you.'

'It's brilliant!' said Fred. 'I've just seen Miss Dunbar and she does the weather 'n' that and she says we're going to have *loads* and it'll be deep enough to sledge in and I told her all about Grandad's sledge.'

Visions of a very athletic grandfather popped into Adelaide's mind. 'Your Grandad's got a sledge?'

'Yup, and he built it for me and Lucy, and it's special.'

'Is it? Why?'

'Cause it's got wheels.'

Adelaide raised her eyebrows. 'Wheels, Fred? In the snow?'

He gave her the look of gentle sympathy he reserved for mere mortals. 'You don't use it with the wheels on when it's snowing, Miss.' He shuffled a little closer. 'The wheels is for after,' he whispered. 'They come off. But it's all right, I won't tell Grandad you didn't know.'

'I appreciate that, Fred. Thank you.'

'That's all right, Miss. Bye!'

The Christmas party at the school was an eagerly anticipated event. Everyone was there as willing volunteers cooked a delicious dinner for the elderly residents of the village. It was a joyous occasion with decorations, crackers, and carols with the church choir. In pride of place stood a large Christmas tree, donated to the village every year by Elias Woodward.

In the kitchen, making tea, Adelaide glanced at the sparkling tree, decorated by the ladies of the WI. It really was one of their best efforts yet, she thought.

The tables were being moved to one side to clear a space in the centre in preparation for Santa's arrival. It was the most popular part of the afternoon with senior citizens and children alike.

'Oh well,' said a voice behind her. 'Here we go. Wish me luck.'

She turned to see curly white hair and beard, and sparkling blue eyes she recognised.

'Good luck,' she whispered. She thought suddenly of Fred. 'Oh, and Nick?'

'Yes?'

'Don't forget the hood.'

He nodded, and flipped up his hood.

One by one the children took the hand of a senior citizen, and they were visited by Santa together. Fred sat beside Florence Garvey, the post mistress long since retired. Florence was sharp and intelligent, with a wealth of knowledge, and even at ninety-one, she could give Mastermind contestants a run for their money.

She had a soft spot for all the children in the village, and Fred was a particular favourite.

'Like minds,' Fred's mother was heard to say. 'She can match him question for question and no explanation is ever too much trouble.'

'Ho-ho-ho! Merry Christmas, everyone!'

Standing behind, Adelaide watched as Santa Nick approached.

'Merry Christmas, Santa,' said Florence and Fred, together.

'Now,' said Santa, reaching into his sack. 'Have you been good this year?'

'Not very, dear,' said Florence. 'But Fred has.'

Adelaide chuckled. Santa gave a loud ho-ho-ho and passed them a gift each.

'Thank you, Santa,' said Fred. 'It won't be my Wii,' he whispered to Florence, as Nick moved on. 'Mum and Dad are getting that. And, anyway, that's not Santa.'

Florence looked at him, keenly. 'Who is it, then?'

'That's Mr Best.'

'Mr Best, your headteacher? Are you sure, Fred?'

'Yup. Mr Wilberforce was Santa last week, but then he broke his ankle, and now he's not, so Mr Best has taken over. I know it's him, 'cause he's got a spot on his nose. He's put something on it, make-up, I expect, but it's definitely the same spot he had the other day, but I won't tell anyone else except you.'

'Well observed, Fred,' said Florence, patting his shoulder.

'I'm good at observing things,' he said, pulling at the paper on his gift. 'It's just natural. Wow! It's a book! I haven't read this one.'

Standing behind them, Adelaide listened. Good try Nick, she thought, but you've been spotted.

The following day was Christmas Eve.

'T'was the night before Christmas,' Adelaide said to herself, as she put pastry tops on several mince pies. She'd been busy for most of the week making mince pies and cinnamon stars to give as gifts to neighbours and friends, and now she was making a few extra, just for herself.

And one for Santa, of course, she told herself. Silly really, but why break the habit of a lifetime?

The pale grey sky was heavy with snow as Adelaide set off to deliver her gifts. At Florence Garvey's front gate, she waited as Fred and his dad finished clearing the path.

'Morning John,' she said. 'Morning, Fred. You're working hard.'

'Yup,' said Fred, shovelling snow.

'Yes,' John said. 'Seemed a good idea to get some fresh air. Doing us both good, isn't it, Fred?'

Fred lifted a huge shovelful of snow and threw it to one side. 'And,' he said, 'me and Lucy are allowed to make a snowman with it after, and we're calling 'im Hercules, and Miss Garvey's finding us a scarf and a hat, and she's going to tell us all about his ten labels.'

John Bunting and Adelaide exchanged glances that said, 'Good luck with that one, Florence.'

As if in answer, Florence opened the door.

'Ah, hello, Adelaide,' she said. 'Thought I heard your voice. I was just going to invite Fred and his dad in for a cup of hot chocolate. Care to join us?'

'Thank you, that would be lovely,' Adelaide said. 'And I've brought you some mince pies and cinnamon stars for Christmas.'

'That is kind of you,' said Florence. 'Come on in and we'll sample them, shall we, Fred?'

The snow was falling again as Adelaide made her way back home, with Fred and his dad.

'Don't forget Boxing Day if you can make it,' John Bunting said, as they went their separate ways.

'Thank you, John,' said Adelaide. 'Have a lovely Christmas Day.'

'You too.'

With a last glance, Adelaide stepped inside and shut the front door. Time for a cup of tea and some toast, and then later she had fish and chips to look forward to. It was a little routine she had for Christmas Eve. Fish and chips on a tray by the fire, watching her favourite films on the television. Bliss.

She felt happy and full of Christmas cheer. Tomorrow, Nick would be round for Christmas dinner, as usual.

Walking across to the fridge, she glanced down the hallway. A tall, willowy shape was clearly visible through the stained glass.

Not Fred, at any rate, she thought. As she walked down the hall, the shape bent to push a card through her letter box.

Adelaide opened the door. It was Clarissa Crochet.

'Oh Adelaide, I'm sorry, I didn't mean to disturb you. Out of a box, I'm afraid.' She passed her the card. 'I enjoy making them normally, but somehow, I couldn't be bothered this year. I joined a pottery class a few months ago, and I just love it. It's the thought that counts, isn't it?'

'Of course,' said Adelaide. 'Would you like to come in for a cup of tea?'

'Oh no, dear, thank you so much,' she said. 'I'm meeting Derek for tea. We met at the pottery class and just seemed to hit it off, you know …'

She gave a shy smile. 'I suppose some people might say it's a bit silly at my age.'

'Not at all,' Adelaide said. 'I hope you have a lovely time, and a lovely Christmas.'

'Thank you, my dear,' Clarissa said. 'And the same to you.'

Adelaide closed the door behind her. Good for you, Clarissa, she thought.

A little later, there was another ring at the bell. Fred was standing on the doorstep, wrapped in a warm coat and scarf. His nose glowed red in the icy air. The snow had stopped and the wind was buffeting the clouds across the sky. A clear, frosty night lay ahead.

'Hello, Miss,' he said. 'I've got a card for you. I made it.'

Adelaide looked up to see Grace Bunting wave from next door's path, where she and Lucy were also delivering cards. Carefully, she opened the envelope. 'Well, thank you, Fred, it's lovely. It will have pride of place on my shelf.'

'Could you please not walk in your snow, Miss, so me and Lucy can make the first footprints in it after Christmas?'

'I promise,' said Adelaide.

'We're having fish and chips tonight,' he said.

'That's lovely. So am I.'

Fred stomped his bright blue wellingtons on the step.

'Santa's not *real*,' he said, 'but I didn't tell Lucy, 'cause she's only little and she's all excited.'

Adelaide looked down at him. Bless him, she thought, he's missing the thrill of believing in Santa.

'You're a good boy, and a good brother,' she said. 'That's not an easy thing to do.' She leaned down to whisper. 'Even though people tell you Santa's not real, you can still believe if you want to, Fred. You know, secretly, all to yourself. People say lots of things are impossible. It doesn't always mean they are.'

'That's what Grandad says, and he knows everything.' A streak of light suddenly caught Fred's eye. 'Miss! Look! It's a shooting star!'

Adelaide watched the dazzling trail soar across the sky. 'So it is.' She sighed. 'How magical.'

Printed in Great Britain
by Amazon